THEY HAD NO ONE BUT EACH OTHER.

They had escaped the most harrowing chase they had ever lived through. And now their relationship had changed. All wariness was gone—and something much deeper had taken its place. For Steven, the luxury of trusting the woman he loved. For Sharmila, trained to suppress all emotion, the relief of letting herself feel. There had been too many other men and too many times when she had lent her body for Israel, but she had discovered another part of herself—a part that belonged not to her country but to herself alone.

THEY WERE A BRITISH AGENT AND A GIRL FROM ISRAELI INTELLIGENCE IN AN ALLIANCE AGAINST THE WORLD.

"A breathless page-turner all the way."

The Buffalo News

Also by Colin D. Peel

NIGHTDIVE

FLAMEOUT

COLIN D. PEEL

PLAYBOY
PAPERBACKS

for
GEORGE and KAY

CHAPTER ONE

For nearly a hundred miles the pall of smoke stretched in a vast purple cloud across the High Sierras. From the adjoining borders of the Kings Canyon National park and the Sierra National forest where the fire had been burning uncontrollably for four days the smoke rose in a great plume from a front now nearly three and a half miles across.

Heading north, driven by the hot August wind, fine particles of carbon dispersed over the High Sierra wilderness area forming an enormous and graceful fan which was dense enough to play strange tricks with the color of the sky.

Streaked irregularly with slashes of red where the smoke thinned towards the horizon, sunset this evening was more than an extraordinary blending of burnt orange and dark blue. It was a sunset of such splendor that those people fortunate enough to witness it would carry the memory with them for many summers. Some of them paused to watch as the colors fused and became steadily deeper, whilst others traveling by car stopped their vehicles beside the road either to take photographs or simply to stand and stare at the magnificent spectacle.

Running roughly parallel with the California-Nevada state border, a sixty mile stretch of highway 395 provided exceptional opportunities to observe the sunset and some of the higher vantage points were crowded with parked cars. Just south of the intersection with route 120 a small layby with space for perhaps half a dozen vehicles was already overfull, several cars having blocked the narrow entry and exit lanes to the area. Sightseers and photographers jostled each other at the railings to obtain the best view whilst a few children played noisily on the grass between the picnic tables. An unusual scene for a late weekday evening and one which could certainly not have been foreseen by the driver of a green Pontiac Firebird which had been parked here for much of the afternoon.

The Pontiac had been driven to this particular spot shortly after midday and only recently had the driver returned to his vehicle after several exhausting hours of walking and climbing in extreme heat and in thoroughly unpleasant country. Astonished and not a little concerned at the sudden popularity of the layby, any admiration which he might have experienced for the sunset was entirely overshadowed by the urgent necessity for him to be on his way at once.

At least three vehicles blocked his exit from the parking area and he should have left here thirty-five minutes ago.

Hemmed in by a Ford on one side and a Dodge pick-up on the other, both of them driverless, the Pontiac might just as easily have been out of gas for all the use it was to him at the moment. With fresh green paint and new number plates it sat there, waiting to be driven those last few miles to Carson City. It had been stolen for him only yesterday.

There were two ways to make the rendezvous in time. Approach the people at the railings and ask for drivers to re-shuffle their cars or sit in the Pontiac and lean impatiently on the horn until the noise destroyed the atmosphere created by the sunset and brought people back to the parking area. Both solutions were unattractive and both would consume precious minutes he could ill afford to squander.

Take one of the other cars. Choose one already facing the road. Perhaps, in his anxiety to obtain a photograph before the light failed, a careless sunset watcher had neglected to remove the keys.

He glanced at his watch. Damn, he thought. Damn the forest fire, damn the sunset and damn Warren Dahl.

Carried downwards by the cooler evening breeze the aroma of burning wood was faintly detectable now. Walking back towards the road he thought that it would be nice to forget. End it all right here. Join the ordinary people staring in wonder at the sky and, if it was not too late, recapture something which he knew after a few more years of this would be lost forever.

None of the cars had been left with keys in the ignition lock.

He returned to the Pontiac, walking quickly and trying to ignore the peculiar color of the horizon. Before he reached the car, gravel crunched under the tires of yet another arrival, probably attracted to the layby he thought by the gathering of vehicles here.

He was slow in turning round, slower to react to what he saw.

Then he was running. Not thirty-five minutes too late —maybe a lifetime.

For a handful of seconds he let the engine idle whilst he computed the angle. And then he made his beginning.

Tires burning on the tarmacadam as the big V8 picked up revs, for ten feet the Firebird accelerated unchecked. It hit the Ford slightly forward of the driver's door, lifting the nose and shoving it bodily several feet to the left. With both front fenders smashed the Firebird scraped horribly between the pick-up and the battered Ford, glanced heavily off the car immediately in front and suddenly was free.

He swung northwards, placed his right foot firmly on the appropriate pedal and let the V8 have its head.

What the hell had gone wrong? Had they spotted the burned out helicopter from the air or had the pilot got a message across before the poor bastard had been incinerated?

Savagely he changed into third, feeling the rear end skip sideways on the curve. Now what? Dahl hadn't bargained on this and even if he could make Carson City with a few minutes' lead there would be no opportunity to hand over the case now.

The other car appeared in his mirror as the Firebird took hold of top gear and began to squat. Lower and lower to the road it sat, the beating of the engine turning gradually into a roar as it began to peak out and the wind noise around the torn fenders sounding as though the whole front of the car was coming apart.

For a further quarter of a mile the Pontiac increased its speed until he knew it had reached the limit. In his mirror the tail car had diminished in size, but not enough. At least the Firebird would give him breathing space and it sounded perfectly healthy—he still had a chance unless they had a radio or a telephone in the car.

Pushing all thoughts but those concerned directly with plain survival to the back of his mind he concentrated on the task of maintaining his slender lead over the black outline of the car behind him.

Experience told him that an outright chase of this kind would provide no more than a thirty or forty per cent chance of complete escape and a hell of a lot less if they were desperate enough to try a few shots on the more deserted stretches of road which lay ahead. In conditions of heavier traffic or on a more twisting road he was confident of his ability to lose them or even sucker them into an accident, but here, on the high altitude plateau of the Sierras, he could no nothing but make sure he stayed in front.

Unlike many of the more powerful cars which have spent dreary lives on the restricted freeways near the coast the Firebird engine did not seem to be choked with accumulated carbon. At an indicated speed of a hundred and thirty-seven he had seen no telltale red sparks from the exhaust and the needle on the temperature gauge had come to rest only three-quarters of its way to the upper limit. There was no dangerous floating from the suspension when the Pontiac swept over depressions in the road, the car feeling surefooted and responding well to the wheel. For a while he was safe. For how long was another question.

Under a darkening sky, now sinister with fifty mile long streaks of crimson against a background of deep purple hues, two tiny specks crawled along the ribbon which was highway 395. To the east, the mountains of Yosemite had already cast their huge shadows across the country and to the west, bordering the highway for nearly two miles, the placid waters of Mono Lake were no longer blue but reflected the strange colors of the dying sunset. Along the empty Nevada border, California began to cool as another summer day faded into night.

Seat belt tight across his chest the occupant of the first car had begun to drive with one hand on the wheel, the other poised ready to punch the headlight switch. Although the road was almost undeviating, at the speed he was traveling, in the twilight, his eyes had already started to deceive him. The shadowy imagined outlines of parked trucks were making his palms sweat and the pursuit car had not lost ground at all.

Also without lights, the car behind him had maintained remarkably constant separation. So much so, that by now he had a nagging suspicion that the driver could close the gap if it were to serve his purpose. The two men he had seen at the layby were driving no ordinary Chevrolet for he knew the Firebird could outrun any standard model regardless of engine size. Instead, he was being followed by a car modified specifically for high speed use—one perhaps which could overhaul the Firebird with comparative ease. The thought did nothing to reduce his tension.

What were they waiting for?

Dahl had been absolutely certain that no one else could know where the helicopter had been brought down. Even though they would have been able to reconstruct its flight path simply enough, it would have been impossible for them to pin point the scene of the accident so quickly let alone get a car on the road from San Francisco. Somewhere, somehow there had been a leak.

Again he forced himself to think of his immediate predicament. If in fact they had discovered that Dahl knew about the transfer, then the car behind might be only one of several sent out to intercept the Firebird. But how the hell had they got the information that had led them to the layby?

He willed another precious five miles an hour out of the roaring engine conscious now of the sweat soaking into his shirt. There was a bitter taste in his mouth and his lips were dry with fear.

Gravel sprayed from the right hand tires as the Firebird drifted slightly off the road surface. At the tremendous speed it was traveling, stones blasted up inside front and rear fenders making a noise like tearing calico.

He flipped the switch flooding the road with light.

Now his followers would have no need of their own headlights. Once darkness fell, in a chase like this the driver in front quickly lost the advantage, having no choice but to advertise his position by tail lights whilst the car behind gradually became swallowed up by the night.

Easing the Firebird into the center of the road to prevent any sudden attempt at overtaking, he strained his vision to the limit of the white swathe cut by the headlights. How close were they?

Half expecting a bullet to punch its way through the

thin sheet metal beside him, he hunched lower in his seat sure now that he was being driven headlong into a trap. Approaching traffic was almost non-existent and he had overtaken only three vehicles since leaving the layby. There had been time enough for them to have made their move.

He reached forward to the glove compartment and withdrew the automatic, checking the safety with his thumb before tucking it into his belt. One thing was certain. The case might not get to Carson City but the two men who were sharing this wild ride with him would never lay their hands on it—not whilst he was still alive. That much at least he owed Dahl. Anyway, it wasn't a question of choice—it never was. The security of the case and his own survival were synonymous. To bring the Firebird to rest here out on the highway so that he could hand over the information in exchange for his life was a thought so irrational that it occupied his mind for no more than a fraction of a second. Somehow or other, before the trap closed, he was going to have to make his own move.

Past the sterile alkali lakes and past the peaks of those mountains which in another time had escaped the relentless scraping of glacial ice, the Firebird flew northwards through the night as if guided by the thin yellow line rushing beneath its belly.

Three hundred yards behind, connected to it by an invisible thread, another car, almost equally invisible in the dark, shadowed the Pontiac waiting patiently for it to reach the small road leading eastwards to the ghost town of Bodie. The trap had indeed been well laid.

At a speed in excess of two miles a minute, the Firebird was less than ninety-two seconds away from sudden death when the driver switched on the interior light to glance at his map. Some sixth sense was urging him to abandon this furious drive right now.

No stranger to circumstances in which his life depended on one single right decision, he had learned not to ignore the vague inner feelings of disquiet which so often preceded the unexpected.

Let them show their hand. See if he had lost his touch or if this was the time for him to become another one of Dahl's numbers.

He eased his foot from the accelerator allowing the car to slow to ninety before applying the brakes. Eighty—seventy—sixty. At fifty he screwed his eyes shut and willed the irises to expand. He counted six seconds, switched off the headlights and opened his eyes wide to the blackness of the windshield.

Wrenching at the wheel he brought the Firebird back to the pale yellow center line of the road and changed down into second. Filling his mirror the grim reflection of the other car was quite clear. They were very close, only feet behind. After the wind and engine noise of a moment ago it was extremely quiet. The automatic slid easily into his hand.

Half a mile ahead at the intersection, a man kneeling uncomfortably on the roof of his station wagon removed his hands from the warm grips of a tripod mounted Masden machine-gun and picked up his radio. The message he received was cut short by a series of extraordinary events taking place a short distance down the road. All too soon the consequences of the interruption were to be of great importance to him.

His instructions had been extremely simple. Wait for a fast moving car to enter the sights of his weapon, aim eighteen inches above the headlights and, once the target was in range, squeeze the trigger. The target, he had been told, would be traveling at a speed in excess of a hundred miles an hour pursued by two of his colleagues in an unlit car a suitable safe distance behind.

To pass the time he had been practicing dry firing at the occasional vehicle which had passed the intersection and was by now confident that even at a hundred miles an hour he could not possibly fail in his mission.

But no sooner had the lights of another vehicle appeared at the beginning of this stretch of the highway than they had mysteriously vanished. Simultaneously he had received the garbled radio message which had served to both alert and confuse him.

He could hear them now and there was the sudden sound of gunshots. Things had not gone well for the driver of the Firebird. He had spun the car expertly enough, no mean achievement at fifty miles an hour in the dark, and he had succeeded in evading the swerving pursuit car as it slipped by. He had even had time to rest his hands against the windshield pillar and squeeze off a couple of hurried shots. But curiously the driver of the Chevrolet had refused to accelerate out of trouble and, although his speed had increased marginally, he had nevertheless managed to avoid switching on his lights.

Steadying his hand for another shot, the driver of the Firebird floored his accelerator to narrow the gap. He must finish it now—quickly and cleanly.

At the same time, knowing he was already dangerously close to the intersection the other driver slammed on his brakes preferring to risk a bullet from behind than certain death from the machine-gun silently waiting for its victim to appear.

A plan of elegant simplicity had gone terribly wrong.

The driver of the Pontiac just had time to hit his headlight switch before the Firebird emblem smashed violently into the rear of the stationary car ahead.

The squeal of shearing metal and the shriek of rubber on the road were drowned by the awful stutter of the Masden.

From the brief flash of the Firebird's headlights the man with the machine-gun had been able to draw his bead. Like other men on this fatal night he too had made his decision.

Trapped in the lead car, less than twenty yards from the intersection, the two occupants in the front seat of the Chevrolet were killed instantaneously.

Bleeding profusely from the mouth, barely conscious after the crash, the driver of the Firebird desperately flung himself out of the open door leaving the frayed ends of his snapped seat belt still resting against the squab.

More bullets tore into the shattered remains of the two cars. A fragment of sharp steel flew from one of the wheel rims to embed itself deeply in his stomach.

Coughing horribly he raised his gun and emptied it at the muzzle flash from the machine-gun.

Still firing, the barrel of the Masden slowly sank until bullets chopped downwards through the thin roof of the station wagon.

Before he died he saw the gunner illuminated in the cruel glare of orange flame which erupted from the punctured gas tank.

There had been no mistakes yet there had been many. There had been four men, now there were none. Four skilled men, all of them knowing the risks and all of them believing implicitly that they would beat the odds yet another time—four men who had died together on this lonely highway and one man who had died alone when his helicopter exploded high over the desert several hours ago. Men expended like so many pawns in the bloody game of international espionage.

Far to the south the forest fire was no longer out of control, the moderating wind having given the rangers an opportunity to halt the advance at the fourth bull-dozed fire-break they had cut. Smoke still billowed from thousands of ruined acres to feed the enormous cloud hanging in a thick fragrant shroud over eastern California, but a pale, blurred area showed where the full August moon was climbing over the mountains.

High above highway 395, like a moth drawn to the dying flames of the burning station wagon, a single-engined light plane fluttered out of the smoke-filled darkness.

With propeller idling, it drew closer and closer until its wheels were skimming the road surface. It landed silently on the empty highway stopping only a few yards from the place where so much destruction had taken place a moment ago. Less than a minute later it had vanished as quickly as it had materialized.

CHAPTER TWO

Colonel Itzhak Yaacobi stood legs apart on the tiled floor of the shower, letting high pressure water scour the last remaining traces of the Negev desert from his skin. For a full quarter of an hour he forced himself to remain in the steaming cubicle, despite the knowledge that his attractive wife was impatiently waiting for him to join her in bed.

When at last he entered the bedroom much of his fatigue had disappeared but the gnawing anxiety which seemed to have become part of the job was as real as ever.

He really would have to see if they could afford air conditioning, he thought. At this time of year Jerusalem was intolerably hot. The next time he was sent to Washington, perhaps he could arrange for a unit to be brought in from the States.

His wife lay on the bed watching him. Under the single sheet he knew she would be naked, her body as eager as always. After six days in the heat of the Negev observing the tests and six long days explaining he was still confident that the missile performance data had not been irretrievably lost, he was not altogether relaxed.

She sensed his preoccupation. "Can you tell me about it this time?" she asked quietly.

He sat down beside her. "Some of it, but the whole damn thing is classified—only six people know what's going on. I'm sorry it has to be like this."

Clasping the sheet to her, she sat up. "There's no need to be sorry, I've told you before. Israel might not have much but I know we wouldn't have anything if people stopped caring."

He smiled at her. "The Americans have a name for statements like that."

"Only because they can't understand how we feel."

"I'm going to get us both a drink," he said. "Then I'll bring you up to date."

"Then what?"

"Then look out."

When he returned to the bedroom she had put on her housecoat and turned on the fan. He sat down on the bed again.

"Here," he passed the drink wondering if any of the others trusted their wives enough to unburden themselves of information which was supposed to be secret. "Do you really want to listen or are you just being an understanding wife?"

"Both," she smiled at him over her glass. "Now begin."

"You know all about the Kfir—the plane the Americans call Lion Cub?"

She nodded. "That's not secret, it's been in the newspapers."

"No, it's just the first fighter aircraft that Israel has built. We've publicized it deliberately even though it's got an American engine and a French airframe. The secret bit is the armament."

He became suddenly conscious of his wife's breasts under the thin fabric of the housecoat.

"Go on," she said.

"Well, we've also developed a missile specially for the Kfir to carry—I've been watching test firings out in the desert. The missile was designed and built without help from anyone and it's really secret—or it was. Two weeks ago someone broke into the factory where guidance electronics are manufactured and managed to get hold of copies of some drawings describing how the homing system works. My job is to stop the information from getting into the wrong hands. That's all." He drained his glass. "Doesn't sound very exciting, does it?"

"And you're worried," his wife leaned across to him. "I can help with that, put your glass on the table."

An hour and a quarter later, Colonel Yaacobi had to admit that the whole matter seemed more in perspective. He lay comfortably in bed, his mind and body more at rest than had been the case for the past few days.

A man chosen for his ability to organize a particular section of MOSSAD, Israel's Intelligence Agency, he had a reputation for toughness and had achieved a good deal of success on other difficult assignments. Much of the Colonel's accomplishment was well deserved. He had a fertile brain and an excellent working knowledge of the intricacies of espionage on a world scale gained in the hard school of West Germany. The remainder of his success came from the coolness and self-assurance which he invariably displayed in public. For this he was largely indebted to his wife, a remarkable woman eight years his junior, who, for the ten years of their marriage, had managed to prevent her man from succumbing to the pressures of his job. Itzhak Yaacobi had no illusions of how much he owed to his lovely wife.

He reached out a hand to her, intending to find out if she was yet asleep.

The phone rang destroying his mood.

Calling from the innocuous premises of a small shop located in one of the more squalid areas of Tel Aviv, a man with a soft voice identified himself at once.

For a few seconds the two men spoke, then the Colonel replaced the receiver and lay back on his pillow. So the Americans had recovered the data—or had they?

The telephone message had allayed some of his concern but it was too soon to be sure that his own recovery plan had failed completely. Whether or not another round of Israel's hard fight for survival had been won still depended on the girl, and her job was by no means over yet.

"Is everything all right?" his wife asked drowsily.

"Yes," he replied, squeezing her hand beneath the bedclothes.

He could not have been more wrong.

Whilst Colonel Yaacobi had been relaxing in the privacy of his home in Jerusalem, a strange meeting was taking place in a stately country house just south of London.

Six men sat around an imposing glass-topped table, gathered there to discuss a subject of importance not only to each one of them personally, but also to the governments of three powerful nations.

At one end of the table, a thick-set man dressed in a summerweight gray suit placed well-manicured hands palms down on the blotter in front of him. Directed at a less sophisticated audience the gesture might well have had the desired effect but to the other men in the room it was no more than a thin and unsuccessful attempt to demonstrate intellectual equality.

"Are you going to answer the question?" One of the representatives from the British Foreign Office twirled a pencil idly between his fingers.

The man in the gray suit cleared his throat. "Gentlemen," he said. "Officially, the Federation of Anglo-American Companies cannot accept that any of our members would contemplate an undertaking of the kind you have described."

"And unofficially, Mr. Dryden?" The second representative of the British government put the question acidly.

"Unofficially, the Federation considers it conceivable that some companies could have decided to act unwisely in their own interests, but I regret I have no direct information which would be of assistance."

A short silence was broken by a rude snort from a very large man seated alone on one side of the table. As chairman of the meeting, John Reylord had become progressively more annoyed at the attitude of the FAAC president as the meeting had dragged on. It was time he used his authority.

He stood up, stubbed out his cigarette and cast his eyes round the table. "No wonder the world is in such a wretched mess," he said quietly, "when all we can do is sit here and play question and answer as though we're a bunch of bloody politicians. Now you listen to this"—he pointed his finger at no one in particular and picked up a red covered file.

"This is the 1976 boycott list issued by the Arab oil states," he said. "It contains the names of over fifteen hundred companies, organizations and individuals who the Arabs refuse to do business with because, one way or another, they're involved with Israel. Some of the names in here are almost household words; the Ford Motor Company, the Xerox Corporation, Helena Rubenstein, Club Mediterranee—you already know them. But there are hundreds of others that most people have never heard of.

"Now, since early in the 1975 recession, every major trading company in Britain and the United States has been clamoring to do business with some of the richest people in the world now—the Arabs. Companies on the blacklist have been losing out on trade and profits in a big way, and numbers of them have been attempting to get their names removed for years. Xerox and Ford have been trying since 1966. Some of them don't even know what their relationship with Israel is supposed to be, which makes it damned near impossible."

John Reylord, senior energy adviser to NATO and

elected American-born chairman of this meeting, paused to light another cigarette. Aware that he was making a second introduction, he knew he was going to have to start from scratch to get the answers he wanted. He began talking again immediately.

"Eighteen days ago, British Intelligence received a tip-off about a consortium of twelve Anglo-American Companies who had taken an original and enterprising step to re-open negotiations with the Arabs. As far as we can determine, these companies launched a private project to steal an extremely valuable military secret from Israel—an undertaking which Israel subsequently confirmed as being entirely successful. The idea behind it, of course, was extremely simple. Hand the information over to the Arabs in exchange for a resumption in unrestricted trade for the companies concerned."

At this point in Reylord's address, Lance Dryden felt it necessary to repeat that no company belonging to his Federation could be involved in such a scheme. He had uttered no more than three words when Reylord turned on him.

"Mr. Dryden," he said coldly. "I must insist that you allow me to finish what I am saying. I am sure we are all anxious to hear your valuable opinions but we must be patient—I will not take much more of your time."

Reylord sat down and continued. "Naturally both British and American governments have been committed to recovering the data and I am pleased to tell you that ten minutes before this meeting began, I received a communication directly from Washington saying they have secured what appear to be the stolen documents. I understand they were intercepted somewhere in California before they had reached their final destination. Thus we have prevented these unscrupulous companies from completing their deal, but of course our job is unfinished, gentlemen. We have yet to discover the names of the organizations involved and we have to take the necessary steps to stop this from ever occurring again."

Reylord stared at each of the other men in the room, meeting their eyes one after another. "Now, before we begin again, let me make one thing quite clear. I want no evasion, no polite mouthings. We are here to work and by God I mean to get things moving."

A quietly spoken man with a sallow complexion opened a file in front of him and began reading from a long list of names.

An uninformed visitor to the meeting would have been astonished to learn of the many American companies blacklisted by the Arab nations. One by one, the names of major corporations were read out, including those previously mentioned by Reylord in his introduction. In all, sixty-eight were named, the last being the huge Coca-Cola organization.

The man closed his file. "Sixty-eight United States companies," he said. "Each one has been thoroughly examined by the CIA in the last two weeks. None of them are involved." He smiled briefly. "I regret that even the CIA cannot carry on with such an enormous task."

Without being asked, one of the British officials produced a similar but rather shorter list of United Kingdom based companies. Reylord prevented him from reading it.

"A process of elimination is not only time consuming," he said, "it is futile and shows a complete lack of imagination by whoever originated the investigations. We must begin at the other end of the scale, gentlemen. Now, Mr. Dryden, would you be good enough to tell us what measures your Federation intends to implement to unearth these companies?"

Dryden sat back in his chair. "It's not the job of the Federation I'm afraid," he said. "Surely, now the documents are safe the matter can be dropped."

Reylord's eyes glinted dangerously. "Unless I get

your full co-operation," he said icily, "with the blessing of the President of the United States and with the full approval of the Prime Minister, I will personally see to it that the Federation of Anglo-American Companies is torn into shreds and that its officers are publicly crucified. Do I make myself clear, Mr. Dryden. This is not a case of fraud or an inquiry into some minor transgression of a trading agreement—this is an international scandal which could easily have had a profound and possibly tragic effect on the Middle East situation. We are discussing espionage, Mr. Dryden, not import tariffs."

The face of the FAAC president became pale, leaving two patches of color high on the cheeks.

"I don't see quite what—in the circumstances," he said lamely, his composure totally destroyed by Reylord's attack.

A colleague of the sallow-faced American who had read from the list addressed the chairman. "Mr. Reylord," he said. "May I suggest the CIA follow up on the information which allowed them to recover the data. One phone call and I can put a hundred men into California." He smiled confidently.

Reylord had no particular wish to continue being unpleasant. He chose his words with care. "I was led to understand that it was the California State police who found the documents," he said. "A CIA man was found dead nearby. It seems there are some rough games being played in our country—but of course much is at stake. I believe the CIA will already be more than heavily involved, but naturally any additional assistance you could arrange can only be to our advantage."

The American nodded. "And the British are also supplying men?"

"That is correct." The man from the Foreign Office answered making it obvious that he considered it unnecessary to elaborate further.

A farce, Reylord thought. A complete bloody farce. The people in the States had no intention of co-operating with the British and the British had no intention of co-operating with the Americans. And Dryden was interested only in protecting his own skin. Why the hell had he landed this one?

He thought briefly of the summer vacation he was missing and of the slender woman with the dark hair he had met at the party last Thursday in New York.

It was nothing but luck that the Israeli drawings had been found in time—either that or somewhere there were other men in authority who really cared about this rotten mess.

John Reylord's assessment of the situation was only partly correct. Like Colonel Yaacobi, he understood the importance of what he was trying to do, but for Reylord there was a further complication.

Only too well he appreciated the value of the Israeli drawings to western nations threatened by the Arab oil embargo, and he knew it was possible that some bright bastard might like to officially leak the drawings of the missile electronics to the Arabs as part of a good-will package. The Jews had neglected to maintain adequate security at their factory and had paid the price. It would be simple enough for some devious politician in Washington or London to hand over the recovered data to Jerusalem whilst at the same time sending copies to the Arabs. Israelis and Arabs would be equally grateful—a desirable state of affairs for both North America and Europe.

One thing Reylord was sure of—he wanted no part of a deal like that. The unnerving thought that, in all probability, he would never know if he were to be involved in an international double-cross had been worrying him ever since he had arrived in England.

An hour later when the meeting had finally adjourned, he left the building to find a fine drizzle sweeping across the empty car park.

Tired, dissatisfied with the results of the meeting and more sure than ever that he was in danger of foundering in unexpectedly deep water, he drove back to his London hotel. He was looking forward to a drink.

Ten minutes after he had arrived his spirits had risen. After all, the Americans had located the stolen documents before anything serious had taken place. As co-ordinator of the exercise he had achieved that much at least.

Like Colonel Yaacobi far away in Jerusalem he, too, could not have been more wrong.

CHAPTER THREE

The impatient blare of a horn behind him made Steven Marsh jump. For the second time in less than a mile he had nearly fallen asleep at an intersection whilst waiting for the lights to change.

He coaxed his rented Volkswagen the last few hundred yards to the motel entrance, turned into the car park and wearily switched off the engine.

Away from the artificial glitter of the strip, the lights of the motel were welcome enough. Las Vegas might not have much class, Marsh thought, but you could rely on even the most modest motel having a gloriously cool bedroom.

Even the floodlights could not completely spoil the magnificence of the Nevada night sky. Marsh walked to his unit, head inclined towards millions of sparkling stars, the extreme clarity of the desert air making them appear brighter than he had ever seen them in England. Only twice before could he remember them being like this, once in Finland and once on a long cold night spent in northern Canada many years ago. Despite the hot night air the memory made him shiver.

Entering the unit was like opening the door of a refrigerated cold store. Without turning on the light, he tossed his flight travel case on to the chair, stretched out on the bed and lit a cigarette. Filtering through the half-open slats of the window blinds, yellow light from the car park formed a striped pattern on the far wall. Letting the cool air gradually reduce his body temperature, Marsh drew hungrily on the cigarette whilst he allowed himself the luxury of thinking of absolutely nothing.

A second later he became shockingly aware of his foolishness. Stars, recollections of Canada—Christ, what had he been thinking of.

Very slowly he moved a hand under his back, sliding it into the pocket of his cords until he could feel the grip of his gun. His other hand snaked out towards the switch on the bedside lamp. The cigarette remained glowing between his lips.

Muscles bunched, Marsh lay on the bed waiting and listening.

Then in one smooth movement he was crouching on the floor, his eyes temporarily blinded by the light.

His sudden exertion had been unnecessary. The room was empty. Marsh stared at the mess of upturned drawers, ripped carpet and slashes in the mattress. So it had begun already—and he was stupid to believe he had got away with it.

Gun in hand, he stood up and moved warily to explore the bathroom and toilet, finding them similarly unoccupied.

Returning to the bedroom, he picked up the phone and asked the receptionist to get him a San Francisco number.

The girl who answered asked him politely if he wanted the export division.

"Barbed-wire," Marsh told her. "Mr. Dahl, please."

"It's gone ten-thirty, sir. Mr. Dahl is not at the office."

"Could you call him at his home for me?" Marsh asked. "It's important. I'd like him to telephone me immediately." He read out the motel number from a card affixed to the wall. "Tell him Steven Marsh is having trouble with an order."

He retrieved his smoldering cigarette from a burnt

patch on the carpet and wandered back into the bath-room.

In the mirror a tired man stared back at him. At thirty-two, Marsh thought, he looked more like some-one already in his early forties. He gave himself the benefit of the doubt and settled on thirty-nine.

An unruly mop of fair hair still gave a faint impres-sion of youth but the slightly gaunt face and the lines at the corners of his eyes showed the years of strain. A face of a man who had lived a trifle hard or who had perhaps suffered a little. But what the hell did it matter.

He stripped off his shirt revealing a lean brown body disfigured by a scar running from his right shoulder blade to his navel. Whilst he was rinsing his face the telephone rang.

Not bothering with a towel, he re-entered the bed-room and picked up the receiver. It was Dahl.

"Sorry to bother you," he said, "but I thought the CIA might like to know someone took the trouble to go through my motel room."

The reply did not surprise him.

"I didn't expect you to do anything about it," he answered calmly. "For all I know you arranged it."

On the other end of the line Warren Dahl swore under his breath. "Why the hell would I do that," he inquired, wondering if the answer might confirm some of his suspicions of Marsh.

Marsh grinned to himself. "How would I know," he said, "I'm just a visitor, remember. All the way from little old England to help out our American cousins. But I don't like my room being searched when I'm out —perhaps you could tell your friends for me."

"You're talking to the wrong department, Marsh," Dahl answered. "You must have upset someone— don't worry about it."

"Nice to know you care," Marsh said. "Now I'm going to carry on with my holiday and I want to be able to enjoy it, so keep out of my hair, Dahl. Don't forget you're supposed to be co-operating."

Dahl managed to keep his voice level. *"We* are supposed to be co-operating," he said. "Both of us—you remember that. And before I say good night you might be surprised to hear we found a bomb in the Firebird."

"Dangerous people the Americans," Marsh said. "Maybe the same person left one in my room. I'd better look."

"One more thing, Marsh."

"What's that?"

"If you find one don't call me, I'm going to bed."

Steven Marsh replaced the receiver still grinning. He was almost sure Dahl hadn't arranged for his unit to be ransacked, even though the CIA had found the explosives he had placed in the Pontiac yesterday morning. Unfortunately that meant his scheme had been discovered by someone else. It hadn't taken them long.

Picking up the phone again he asked the girl at the desk if half a bottle of Scotch could be brought to his room. "For the price of two full bottles," he explained. "I'm sure you can find one somewhere."

Ten minutes later, Marsh was seated comfortably in an easy chair, a fresh packet of cigarettes and an unopened bottle beside him on the table. He had some heavy thinking ahead of him.

Steven Marsh had arrived in the United States only twelve days ago. In such a short time he seemed to have accomplished everything he had hoped for—but that was before he had found his room had been searched. Now the situation had suddenly taken a different twist. A twist he had not foreseen and one which could have very serious consequences if he proved unable to get to the bottom of it in a hurry.

Employed by an obscure offshoot of British Intelligence, Marsh had been engaged—a word coined by the five men who worked in the department—three years ago to investigate the suspected theft of components from one of Britain's largest military research establishments.

His somewhat direct and unusual method of operating had not endeared him to the shadowy men who control the more important aspects of Britain's destiny, but it was generally, if reluctantly, acknowledged that Steven Marsh was an agent of exceptional ability. Such a sweeping recommendation—when made, which was rarely so—was invariably tempered by remarks concerning his weakness for women and his sublime disregard for authority. Nevertheless, for this assignment, there had been no other choice. Until half an hour ago the talents of Steven Marsh had not been over extended. Even now, if they had known about it, the unexpected turn in events would not have made his employers in London reconsider the wisdom of their selection.

With detailed information concerning the recent efforts of twelve unknown Anglo-American companies dedicated to the furtherance of profitable trade with the oil rich Arabs, Marsh had soon been working with the CIA in San Francisco.

Although forewarned in England, Marsh had quickly become uneasy at the internal security of the American agency. The sorry series of political scandals which racked the United States in the mid-seventies had undermined what was once one of the world's most powerful undercover organizations and he had found the CIA nervous and even anxious to communicate their intentions to Washington.

Rightly, he had concluded that the CIA plan to snatch the Israeli drawings from a private helicopter flying to San Francisco from Salt Lake City was doomed to failure. Too many conflicting interests were represented in Washington and too many ears in the nation's capital were waiting for the CIA to announce their proposal.

Suspecting that Dahl's agent would be intercepted

either before or after he had shot down the helicopter over the Californian desert, Marsh had wisely made his own arrangements. And, like the majority of his outrageous and frequently dangerous plans, they had succeeded.

He poured himself another generous measure of whisky and lit another cigarette from the glowing butt of the one between his fingers.

Everything had worked out perfectly last night, he thought. The twelve companies had hired a pretty tough outfit to do the job, but he had still beaten them at their own game. That he had been lucky there was no doubt—if last night had turned out differently he could easily have had to try stopping their Chevrolet with the hand grenades he had carried in the plane, or, alternatively, tail the car for hours until it had arrived at its destination. But Marsh was used to being lucky.

The small packet of explosives which he had wired to the rear axle of the Firebird had been no more than insurance. If Dahl's driver had managed to elude the two men in the Chev, Marsh would still have been the winner. Although of no consequence now, he was glad his insurance had not been used.

Recapturing the violence of last night, Marsh thought things were definitely warming up.

So far, he had been making the running—now someone else had stepped in.

Who could know the British Government had instructed him to prevent the CIA from getting hold of the Israeli information? And who could know he'd substituted a complete set of false drawings for the ones he had stolen from the shattered remains of the Firebird out there on the highway. Not the CIA, he thought —they would be happy with the ones they'd just recovered and that should keep them out of his hair for long enough.

He levered himself out of the chair and walked to the window. Someone, somewhere, knew he was the

owner of the genuine information. And they were waiting.

The lubricating qualities of the Scotch could not
combat the rough dryness in his throat. Two days of
too many cigarettes combined with an almost total lack
of sleep were having their effect. But he was no longer
tired, his weariness having been pushed aside for a few
more hours whilst he grappled with yet another set of
problems.

Shortly before midnight, very little further ahead
with his reasoning but with sufficient Scotch inside him
to make sleep a real possibility, he started to undress.

He was prevented from climbing into bed by the
unexpected ringing of his telephone.

The girl's voice was not that of the motel receptionist, nor that of Dahl's secretary in San Francisco. "Mr.
Marsh?" she inquired, "Mr. Steven Marsh?"

Quickly he turned off the table lamp and carried the
telephone away from the window. "That's right," Marsh
answered. "Good evening."

"Mr. Marsh, I'm sorry to call so late but I haven't
had the opportunity since ten-thirty and you were out
before that."

Not an American, Marsh decided, and not English
either. The voice had a well-disguised accent and a
peculiarly rich quality about it.

"It's perfectly all right," Marsh assured her. "I hadn't
gone to bed."

"I need to speak to you rather urgently. You are
alone?"

Not "are you alone," Marsh noted, but the reversal
of the first two words told him nothing he had not already established.

"Yes, I am, it's quite safe to talk," he said.

"I would prefer to meet you if it is possible."

"Now?"

"There is a restaurant at the corner of Tahoe Boulevard where it meets the Whitney road. Could you be there in—?"

Marsh interrupted her. "I haven't any transport," he lied.

"You could take a taxi, maybe. It is very important."

"Or you could come here to the motel."

There was a moment's silence.

"It is very late," she said hesitantly, "and I know you have a car."

And I know that you know, Marsh thought.

"I didn't say I haven't got a car," he said. "My Volkswagen decided to fuse its lights earlier tonight, so I'd rather you came here if it's that urgent."

There was a sigh from the receiver. "Mr. Marsh," she said, "please stop it. I saw you arrive at the motel and there's nothing wrong with your headlights. I'll be with you in fifteen minutes. That'll save us arguing, won't it."

"I'll be waiting," Marsh answered cheerfully. "Good-bye."

Fifteen minutes. Not long enough and anyway he was tired of thinking. If it was a trap it was unlikely that he would have received any advance warning. He would wait and see.

His curiosity aroused, he made certain the venetian blinds were fully closed then busied himself by clearing up some of the mess left by his earlier visitors. From his case he took a bottle of pills swallowing two of the tiny tablets with the dregs of whisky in his glass. At once he could feel the stimulant begin pushing his drowsiness away.

At ten minutes past midnight the floodlights in the car park were abruptly extinguished. Surely nobody bothered in Las Vegas, Marsh thought, power saving in this part of the world was inconceivable.

Struggling into a clean shirt he picked up the phone, half expecting it to be dead.

"Yes, sir?" It was the receptionist.

"Do you always turn off the lights in the car park?" Marsh asked her pleasantly. "It's just that I have a visitor arriving shortly."

"I'm sorry, sir—they're on an automatic time switch. I'll see if I can find the key and over-ride it."

Car headlights shone briefly on the outside of the plastic blinds.

"It's okay," he said. "Don't bother, she's here now. Sorry to be a nuisance—good night."

"Good night, sir, I hope you enjoy your visitor."

Marsh couldn't suppress a smile at the remark. He picked up his gun from the bed and flicked off the safety.

Three gentle taps on the door were followed by a girl's voice saying, "Mr. Marsh," in a loud whisper.

"Come on in," Marsh said, "it's not locked."

The slim young woman who entered the room was quite unlike anyone Marsh had seen before. Dressed in tight flared jeans and an equally tight fitting white polo necked sweater made of some thin material, it was her face which was exceptional. Long shoulder length, dark brown hair falling across one cheek and two very large brown eyes were the most obvious features, but it was the girl's mouth which seemed to make her so different from a thousand others drifting through Las Vegas on a summer night.

Smiling very slightly, her eyes were fixed on the gun in Marsh's hand. "You would like me to lock the door?" she asked. "Then you'll be able to put that down."

She really was beautiful, Marsh thought. Where the hell had she come from? And where did she fit in all this?

He returned the smile. "Allow me," he said, walking towards her, his gun held loosely at his side. Still facing her, he reached over her shoulder with his left arm to click the catch and slide the chain latch into its slot. During the entire maneuver his eyes never left hers.

Although he was very close to her she made not the slightest attempt to move back and the smile remained on her lips. He could feel her breath on his face.

Before he withdrew his arm she began to turn, lifting both her arms high above her head until she was facing the door. She placed her palms against it leaning forwards waiting for him to search for a gun.

"Another child of Zion—far from home," he said softly.

She spun round the smile gone.

Marsh threw his gun on to the bed. "Only a guess," he said, "but a good one as it turned out. Come and sit down."

Slipping out of her sandals she walked across the room and let herself drop into a chair. "You're not so close to home yourself, Mr. Marsh," she said.

"Steven, you already know my name. Don't call me Mr. Marsh."

"My name's Sharmila Talmai—my real name."

"And you're here on business?"

She nodded at him. "But I'm allowed to drink on duty. Can I have some of that?" She pointed to the half empty bottle of Scotch. "It might wake me up."

"It won't," replied Marsh, "but I'll fix you one."

Not older than twenty-six or seven he decided, and as innocent as a sawed-off shot gun. He wondered if she thought they were both working on the same side. When he wasn't even certain which side he was on himself, there was nothing to be gained in bothering to find out.

She took the glass from him placing her index finger flush with her pretty nose. "You can't tell I'm Jewish," she said.

"No, but I can be fairly certain you're not working for the PLO and you don't look like an Arab, somehow."

"Thank you for that, at least."

"American based or all the way from Israel?" Marsh asked.

"Do you have to know?"

"No," he grinned. "Tell me what you want instead."

"Don't you want to know how much I know first?" She gulped down the Scotch.

"Start talking."

"Well, first of all I know the CIA is all busted open, or at least part of it is. I know you rented an aircraft yesterday afternoon from Reno—a Cessna. You returned it late last night to the same place and I know the CIA have got hold of what they think are the drawings of the Kfir missile electronics—I was told this morning by one of our contacts in Reno."

Steven Marsh thought he must have been particularly careless. Either that or the Israelis were better organized than they had been a year ago. From what she had said already, he had an unpleasant suspicion they might know far too much.

"Clever girl," he said, "go on."

"The next bit's more tricky but more interesting. I've had to guess some of it. The fact that you've been sent all the way out here can only really be explained two ways—either the British distrust the Americans and believe they might not keep our secret, or Britain wants to get its hands on the drawings first."

"I see," he said, "and what about NATO and the common interests of Britain and the U.S.? Don't forget we're supposed to be helping Israel on this one."

She smiled again. "Israel hasn't got any oil, Steven."

Marsh lit a cigarette, offering her the packet as an afterthought.

She shook her head, obviously anxious to continue with her explanation.

"I checked over that Cessna this morning," she said, "very carefully. And I found three patches of blood on the passenger seat and one on the floor."

Marsh said nothing waiting for the punch line. He

realized she was expecting him to say something but he was not absolutely sure yet.

She prompted him. "You've been busy," she said, "haven't you?"

"And you've added two and two together to make twelve," he answered. "What else do you have to tell me?"

She pulled her hair back from her face and looked him in the eyes.

"Nothing really," she said slowly, "but I think you've double-crossed the CIA and that's why I've come here. I can't prove anything—I don't have to. Earlier tonight I came here to see you. Two men were inside your unit looking for something—I watched them through the blinds. Someone else is interested in you, too."

Inwardly Marsh was breathing more easily. A smart, pretty girl—one of Israel's new army assigned to watch him and slice him into pieces if and when it suited her purpose. And she was guessing. Only guessing.

"You're working alone?" he asked.

"More or less."

"First job?"

She shook her head. "You don't get one like this first time."

"Okay," he said, "now tell me what you want?"

She stood up and helped herself to more Scotch. "Israel wants those drawings back, Steven—we want them back before anyone else has the chance to copy them."

"The people who stole them might have already," Marsh said.

"They might, but the Arabs would demand the originals. We'll take a chance with the companies who thought up the idea but we'd rather not take chances with your Government or the White House."

Marsh smiled at her. "So you've come to make a deal with me?"

"Does that mean you really have the information and the CIA doesn't?"

His smile broadened. "That's what makes it so interesting," he said, "for you I mean. You could make me an offer for something I don't have."

She was trying to appear unruffled by his attitude. "Is there any point in me carrying on?"

"With your assignment or the offer?"

"Damn you," her huge eyes flashed at him. "I can go to Dahl."

He stood up and moved towards her. "What good will that do you," he said. "What's the offer?"

"What do you want?"

Reaching out a hand he touched the side of her neck. Her skin was warm and moist. "Just to begin with," he said quietly.

The brown eyes immediately faded and her mouth twisted into another smile. Marsh felt the tendons stiffen in her throat.

"I won't be much good," she said dully, "I'm awfully tired." She turned and walked to the bed. "Somehow I didn't expect you—" she left the sentence unfinished.

Marsh waited until she was two feet away, putting as much strength into the slap as he could muster. It caught her squarely across the backside, the force of it propelling her forward to fall face down on the bed.

He let her lie there, hearing the sobs and conscious for the thousandth time of the rottenness which sent men and women out into the world to wheel and deal for their masters.

When he turned her over gently by the shoulders, her cheeks were wet with tears.

"Coffee," he said; "I'll fix it. Don't go away."

He returned to find her sitting in the chair again. She took the drink from him without speaking.

"You're not what I thought," Marsh said.

"You mean I'm not very good at my job?"

"Yes, but that's a compliment—you're a real person. I'm sorry if I hurt you."

"What's the time, please?"

He looked at his watch. "Nearly one o'clock."

"Can I stay here until morning?" she stared into her cup.

Marsh groaned. "I suppose so, the receptionist was expecting you to, I think. I wouldn't want to spoil my image."

"I'll get my things from the car." She stood up. "Thank you," she said, "for everything. I'll only be a minute." She unlocked the door and slipped out leaving it open behind her.

A second later he heard the scream.

Pausing only to grab his gun, in two bounds he was outside.

The blow from the axe handle caught him neatly just beneath the base of his skull.

CHAPTER FOUR

In the life of every man there are times when a single foolish error causes an unexpectedly dramatic change in his personal circumstances. Failure to observe a road sign when driving at high speed, the decision to have just one more drink or perhaps simply a word said out of place in the wrong company.

For some men the daily avoidance of such minor mistakes is a prerequisite for plain survival and although on this occasion Steven Marsh had escaped with his life, he was fully aware of the stupidity of what he had done. Equally well he knew he had been spared for a purpose.

He had regained consciousness to find himself lying on the rear seat of a rapidly moving car, his head cushioned on the lap of the Israeli girl and his hands and feet securely bound. The back of his head felt as though a fairly large wall had fallen on it.

Extremely dizzy, it had taken him several minutes to reconstruct the events leading up to his capture but one important question still remained unanswered.

Very slowly he began twisting his head on the girl's lap to find out whether he had made one mistake or two. At once, two small hands pressed down gently on his cheek.

Straining to focus his eyes at such close range, Marsh squinted upwards at her wrists to see the tight coils of nylon cord which tied them together. A trick? Persuade him they'd both been taken prisoner and let the girl work on him later? Or was she genuine and not a decoy at all?

He forced himself to try and relax, sensing she was telling him to stay where he was. Jesus, he thought, a successful assignment which had turned into a bloody disaster just as he'd been kidding himself it was all over. And because he had relied on his luck or maybe because he'd become too cocky. This time he'd really blown it. Marsh realized he was frightened.

At a speed he estimated to be in excess of seventy miles an hour the car was traveling on a completely straight road with moonlight streaming through the right hand window. From what little he could remember of the road network surrounding Las Vegas, only one highway led out northwards heading for Reno four hundred and fifty miles away—but the knowledge was of minimal value when he had no way of knowing how long they'd been on the road.

Certain only that he was for the moment helpless in the back of a car being driven to an unknown destination, Marsh thought that it would be nice to be sure Sharmila Talmai was what she seemed.

He moved his head again, more quickly this time so she would know he was fully conscious. The hands left his cheek and Marsh felt a finger touch his lips warning him to remain quiet.

A little less than an hour later, his limbs cramped and his body bathed in sweat, Marsh was approaching the limit of his endurance. Not a word had been spoken by the man or men occupying the front seat and the girl had been similarly silent for the entire journey so far. Perspiration from his face had soaked into her jeans and he knew the weight of his head must be numbing her legs after such a length of time, but she had said nothing nor made any attempt to shift her position. Occasionally, fingers had brushed across his face and more recently she had begun drawing them over his forehead as if to show she understood that he was in pain. He wished he could be sure about her.

Shortly after Marsh decided that, despite her insistence, it was impossible for him to remain bent double on the seat, the car began to slow. Seconds later it swung on to another road, having what he judged to be a sandy or graveled surface. He could wait—for another ten minutes he could wait. In the rear of the car the ride became progressively rougher to the point where it was difficult to prevent himself from rolling off the seat altogether. Marsh could feel the sand tugging at the back wheels now and he suspected he was being driven deeper into the desert along a rarely used track of some kind.

There were voices from the front of the car and then suddenly the journey was over. At once he allowed his body to go limp.

"Out." He heard the instruction directed at the girl and felt her sodden jeans slip from beneath his head.

Hands grabbed him under the arms pulling him roughly from the car. After being compressed for so long it was wonderful to be able to let his heels drag through the sand with straightened legs. Although Marsh was ready to be dropped at any second he managed to stay relaxed as if oblivious to what was happening to him.

When he was finally released he collapsed, not upon a cool bed of sand, but on a floor of particularly unyielding concrete.

Aware of the presence of the girl, he waited to hear the door close before opening his eyes and struggling awkwardly into a sitting position.

A solitary candle flickered on a ramshackle table leaning crookedly against one wall of a tiny room lined with rough-hewn wooden planks. The girl stood with her back against the door, a white figure against a somber background of dark shadows. Her hands were no longer tied.

Marsh held out his wrists to her.

She knelt in front of him using her teeth and nails to untie the knots.

"I wanted to be able to talk to you before they do," she whispered. "That's why I hoped you'd pretend you were still unconscious."

"They're probably listening," Marsh said wearily. "How long were we on the road?"

"Just under two hours," she looked at her watch. "One hour, fifty-six minutes."

With relief he felt the circulation start to return as the nylon slipped undone.

"No, it's okay." He pushed her hands away from the cord on his ankles. "I'll do it."

Still kneeling she turned her head slightly. "You don't trust me," she said, "do you?"

What the hell do you expect," he answered angrily. "When do you seduce the kidnapers and let me escape so I can lead you all to the buried treasure?"

She stood up. "There's nothing I can say, is there?"

"You said you wanted to talk to me before they begin with the clever questions. What did you have in mind?" He threw the nylon into the corner of the room, rose unsteadily to his feet and went to light a cigarette from the candle flame.

"Do you think they really are listening?" she asked quietly.

"Does it matter?"

"Please don't, Steven, I'm sorry it's turned out like this."

"Not as sorry as I am—what do you have to lose? There's an old English saying that women are the devil's net. In my business, it's a saying you make sure you remember. How do I know you haven't arranged all this?"

She looked at the floor. "I wouldn't have agreed to go to bed with you, would I? There would've been no need."

One more nasty push, Marsh decided, and if it provoked nothing to help him make up his mind one way or the other, he'd have to wait.

"I'm not in the habit of trusting Jewish bitches," he said, "and I wouldn't go to bed with one if she had a body a hundred times better than yours and paid me a thousand dollars for my trouble. Think about that, Miss Talmai." He stared hard into the brown eyes and tried to read them, knowing immediately that he had underestimated her.

"And you have just overplayed your hand, Steven Marsh," she said slowly. "Do you think MOSSAD would send me on a job like this if I was stupid? Two hours ago I knew exactly what kind of man you are and it's no use trying to be someone else, you're no good at it. I can understand your distrust but you won't find out anything more by bad acting."

Marsh sighed. "If we'd gone to bed maybe we'd still be there instead of here, wherever here is."

She ignored the remark, reaching out for his hand. "Please listen, Steven, there may not be long and this is important. I've already told you my country will do a deal with you if you have the real drawings. I want you to know what it is before anything happens. Maybe it'll help you to decide something and maybe you'll be able to decide about me."

"Do you also have instructions to sleep with whoever asks you?" Strangely Marsh felt the need to know.

"That's my choice. Never mind that now, just listen. First of all, if you really have the true copies of the Kfir missile drawings, it might be because Britain is as untrustworthy as we think the Americans could turn out to be and we already know it's no good offering you money. I've read a file on you, Steven."

Marsh thought that the Israelis certainly had come a long way in a short time. He drew thoughtfully on his cigarette wondering how complicated this project was going to become. He had an unpleasant feeling that as soon as the door to the room was opened everything might be all too clear.

"Go on," he said, "I might as well hear it."

She lowered her voice and began talking quietly. "In return for the data, Israel will exchange two items of hardware which we think Britain would be interested in. But we won't exchange them with the British Government—only with you—otherwise we have no guarantee that our secret will not be leaked to the Arab nations. Arab oil has made Israel very nervous. Very simply, if you hand over the drawings we'll provide you with information which will help Britain and allow you either to think up an excuse for losing the Kfir missile drawings or to explain to your Government why you made yourself personally responsible for the exchange. Either way, we believe British Military Intelligence would be entirely satisfied."

"And the hardware is?" Marsh inquired interestedly.

"A completely instrumented unused MIG-23 fuselage and a slightly damaged Soviet SCUD anti-tank missile of a type we've not seen before."

Astonished to learn that the Israelis were prepared to trade on such a scale, Marsh pondered on what she had said.

"Wouldn't it be in Israel's interest to give them to the Americans?" he said. "Surely, the more the U.S. can find out about Russian weapons the more able they are to help Israel with arms."

"Britain will send them to the States anyway, once they've analyzed them, but your government would still like to lay their hands on them first. If we can safeguard our own secret for what is a very one-sided deal in Britain's favor, why not do it?"

Here, in this candle-lit prison, a slim Israeli girl was offering Marsh an espionage deal big enough to make many a western mouth water. The unreality of what was taking place was heightened by the very obvious fact that she was a young woman and because of the somewhat dangerous circumstances surrounding them both at this very moment. The package Israel was offering was of such huge significance it seemed unlikely the girl was lying. An exchange of more modest proportions would have been more realistic and Marsh was now inclined to believe she was in reality not only able to speak authoritatively for the Israeli Government but empowered to negotiate a deal of this importance.

"Why didn't you mention this at the motel?" he asked her.

She smiled at him. "You didn't give me a chance—remember. Do you still think I'm a real person?"

"Do you still want to stay the night?"

She glanced around the room. "If you don't mind."

"Okay," Marsh said, "now forget about all that. Have you any idea where we are and who's been kind enough to bring us here?"

"No and no, but they're the same two men I saw searching your motel earlier this evening—at least I think so. It's the same car, anyway."

"Did they say anything to you?"

"Nothing at all but I'm sure they're both Americans —I heard them talk to each other—nothing of any help though."

Marsh lit another cigarette. "You realize someone else must think I've switched the drawings, don't you?"

"No one else could—except the CIA."

Unfortunately, Marsh thought, it probably wasn't the CIA and that only left two other possibilities; someone from his own department in England or whoever was working for the twelve companies. There was one further question he had to ask the girl.

"Sharmila," he said, using her Christian name for the first time, "if you weren't convinced I'd switched these drawings would you have tried to make the same deal with someone from the CIA?"

"I suppose so," she answered. "I've already told

you, Israel wants them back. What are you going to do now?"

To be able to answer her question Marsh needed much more information; information which he knew could only be obtained once he was summoned by whoever had brought him here.

"What's the time?" he asked. "I left my watch at the motel."

"Nearly three-thirty."

He considered the possibility that they would be undisturbed until morning but, in the circumstances, it seemed more likely their captors were waiting only for him to wake up. They could very easily appear at any moment.

Taking the stub of candle from the table he made a close examination of the room, discovering, not surprisingly, that it offered no obvious way of escape. He gave the door an exploratory kick. It was another mistake.

Almost immediately there was the sound of bolts being drawn back and the door opened.

Holding a hurricane lamp, a tall thin man stood silhouetted in the doorway. Without moving, he shouted a name which Marsh could not immediately recognize.

Footsteps announced the arrival of another man. As tall as his colleague, but with a build to match his height, he also stood in the doorway.

"If you're room service," Marsh said pleasantly, "I'd like a club sandwich and a can of cold beer."

"I see Miss Talmai has untied you," the thin man spoke with a slight impediment. "We have some questions for you, Mr. Marsh. Forget the beer and come with me."

Marsh squeezed the girl's hand reassuringly. "Won't be long," he said. "Wait up for me." He could see the fear in her eyes.

Outside the single-roomed cabin which served as

their prison, he considered matching his skill against them both. Although more men could be hidden in the moonlit building he could see ahead of him, if he was quick and silent there was a chance. He abandoned his plan as he felt the warning thrust of a gun barrel in the small of his back.

From behind him, the shadow of the large man joined with his own on the sand.

"Don't do that," Marsh growled, "I don't like it."

The remark drew no comment from his escort.

A derelict farm house, Marsh concluded from a very brief examination of the exterior of the building—or more likely an old prospector's cabin.

Inside, the floor was deep in undisturbed dust and fine sand, giving the impression that this was not habitually used as a headquarters. Why they had brought him so far from Las Vegas was something of a mystery —especially to a place like this.

The hurricane lamp illuminated a room as uncompromisingly stark as the one he had just left. A table, a wooden trestle and three ancient chairs added to the general air of decay and desertion.

Indicating that he should sit down on one of the chairs, the thin man placed the lamp on the table, his sallow face appearing grotesque in the shadows cast by the harsh light.

Marsh lit a cigarette, forcing his hands to remain steady. "Okay," he said, "who are you and what's your problem?"

It was the large man who opened the inquiry. He wasted no time in preliminaries. "Where are the Israeli drawings of the Kfir missile electronics, Marsh?" he said bluntly. "The real ones."

Marsh blew a stream of smoke from his mouth then launched into an original and highly colored description of the ancestry of the man who had asked the question.

A trace of annoyance flickered transiently across the

features of the thin man. "Don't be dumb," he lisped, "or even pretend to be. We can start kicking you around right now if that's how you want it—just say the word."

"Let's get something straight right away," Marsh said. "I don't do business with people who bang me over the head late at night. If you want to talk intelligently—which doesn't mean asking stupid questions—then I might listen—but you decide."

Marsh had learned nothing of any value yet and, unless he could prompt them into some sort of negotiation, it was quite on the cards they could start getting tough right away.

"Who do you represent, gentlemen?" Marsh inquired.

Lips compressed in a tight line, the thin man was coming towards him in much the same way as a snake travels over smooth sand. Marsh made ready his defense, wondering if his opponent would use only his hands.

Impending violence was prevented, temporarily at least, by a word of command from the man who had remained seated.

"Marsh," he said. "There is no reason for me to say anything to you at all. However, if it will accelerate matters I am prepared to make our position clear. My friend and I are responsible to the industrial concerns who wish to have their names removed from the Arab boycott list—I am sure you know the background perfectly well.

"Two days ago someone interfered with our plans —someone who was not expected to add such an irritating complication—you, Mr. Marsh. Before that, the CIA attempted to recover the drawings by destroying our helicopter. Fortunately, we were notified in time and, but for an accident, the drawings would by now be safely delivered.

"For some hours afterwards we were under the impression that the drawings had been irretrievably lost to us and once again in the hands of the CIA. Then, Mr. Marsh, something very interesting happened. One of our men had been watching an Israeli girl who we believed to be in the States for reasons not unconnected with our project. She began telephoning you yesterday evening at very frequent intervals. As a precaution, and to make sure we had not missed anything, we paid a visit to your motel in Las Vegas where we installed a radio transmitter. There is, I'm sure, no need for me to continue."

"No," Marsh agreed, the sinking in his stomach having stopped when it reached his knees. "But I'm afraid you're wrong, too. Miss Talmai is under the impression that I have the real drawings as well but so far neither of you seem to have considered how the hell I could have arranged it, let alone why I'd want to."

"Ah, but the girl did mention the aircraft, and her suspicion of both American and British Governments is, in our estimation, entirely justifiable. I am quite confident you are working solely for the U.K., Mr. Marsh, and not in the joint interests of both our countries nor of NATO."

"So you've brought me here to persuade me to give the drawings back to you," Marsh said. "I'm sorry you've gone to so much trouble—you'll have to go back to your spies in the CIA and try again. I haven't got them."

The thin man had listened to the conversation without returning to his seat. He seemed agitated and anxious to say something.

Marsh looked at him. "Don't look so unhappy," he said, "you should've done the job right to start with."

A sharp click told Marsh what he wanted to know. Very slowly he rose to his feet and adopted a slight crouch, hands ready in front of him.

"Come on then," he whispered, "let's see how good you are."

For a fraction of a second Marsh watched the point of the knife, then riveted his attention on the tiny close-set eyes of his opponent waiting for them to announce the first sudden sweep of the blade.

"Where are the drawings?" The lisp was more pronounced.

Marsh sprang sideways, realized he'd been fooled and made ready to parry a thrust.

Faster than he could follow, the thin man was changing knife hands with such dexterity that the blade was no more than a dull blur. He began to sweat, knowing he had misjudged his adversary. Poised on his toes, Marsh prepared to fight for his life.

For the second time he leaped, saw the flash of steel too late and braced himself for the inevitable cut.

A thud between his feet told him that he was being played with. Buried almost to its hilt, the knife quivered in the rotten floorboards.

The thin man retired to the other side of the room, leaving the knife where it was.

"Only a careless man would make the invitation you did," he said. "But you're quick, Marsh. Later we will see if you are quick enough. Next time you will start with the knife, it will be more interesting for you."

Still sweating, Marsh reached down and pulled the blade from the floor knowing there was a gun trained on him from the moment he began to move.

"Keep it, Mr. Marsh." The big man spoke. "In two hours' time at daybreak before it is too hot it may prove useful to you. Are you sure you don't want to answer our question?"

"I'm sure," Marsh said grimly. "I've already told you, I haven't got the answer."

"Would you like us to fetch the girl, Marsh? My friend is very skilled with girls, he uses a small knife only two inches long."

Marsh's skin crawled. "Help yourself," he said casually. "She thinks I've got the drawings, too—you're all a bloody nuisance. Do what the hell you like."

Initially Marsh had decided that the well-built man was the more intelligent of the two and he had appeared to be the spokesman as well as less obviously aggressive. Now he knew he was dealing with a pair of cruel professionals.

Probably trained in one of the violent city environments of North America, the breeding ground for numerous men like these, Marsh had no illusions of what he was up against. Hired at enormous cost to carry out the U.S. side of the enterprise, they would be interested only in completing the job whilst deriving as much miserable enjoyment from it as they could.

He studied them more closely. Well educated but short on conscience the large man would be reliable and as ruthless as his vicious friend, Marsh thought, a combination as effective as it would be unpleasant.

"You have an hour." The thin man spoke in his lisp again. "By then it will be light enough. If you haven't changed your mind we have a way of doing it for you. I've never seen it fail, Marsh. It is the way of the desert." His face twisted into a mask. "And afterwards we'll try the Jew and see what she can tell us."

Marsh moved the knife in his hand.

"I wouldn't kill you—not before you talk." The gun glinted in the fist of the large American. "You can go back with the girl now. You are a stupid fool, Marsh, but we are used to dealing with fools."

In very different situations Steven Marsh had been threatened before. He had been beaten insensible on numerous occasions and, two years ago, four industrious gentlemen in Athens had worked on him for over an hour in an attempt to persuade him to divulge a telephone number. The memories and scars of these encounters, he knew, would never leave him but never in the past could he recall being so unreasonably frightened of the immediate future. This was going to be the time when he came completely unstuck and he had a whole hour in which to savor it. Out here in the desert, no one was going to pull him out of this one.

He was very nearly right.

CHAPTER FIVE

Dawn. For creatures of the desert the inevitable return of the Nevada sun to again bake sand and scrub after the welcome coolness of the night. A time for living things to retreat to their homes deep in the ground before temperatures reached levels which would maim or kill any one of them left on the surface without shade.

In the morning shadow of the Pahute Mesa, four and a half miles inside the western boundary of the Las Vegas bombing and gunnery range, four people stood outside a bleached wooden house waiting for the first rays of sunshine to wash across the sand.

For one of them, this was to be no ordinary morning. Today, Steven Marsh was not ready for daybreak.

"Where did you get this cute idea from?" he asked.

From his side, the girl ran suddenly forwards to shout at the two men leaning idly against an enclosure of corrugated iron. "You can't—you're not human. Animals!" She spat at the feet of the thin man.

"Leave it, Sharmila," Marsh instructed. "Let them have their fun." He willed himself to speak calmly.

No choice, no chance. Not a single bloody way out unless he told them everything and even then was there really a chance? All the time he could keep them on the hook they'd have to keep him alive. Once they'd learned where the drawings were his usefulness would vanish and Marsh was certain his own survival depended only on holding out for as long as he could—however long that might prove to be.

They were expecting him to make a last minute bid for freedom and when he did—if he did—they would shoot him in the legs before pushing him inside there. He wondered how it was going to be when the door closed behind him.

"Sharmila," Marsh called to her, watching her walk back to him, a slip of a girl caught up in something no one should have to watch.

"Tell them," she said. "For God's sake tell them."

Marsh shook his head. "If I do we're both dead—this way we gain a little time. You never know, the Cavalry might arrive. Anyway, don't write me off so easily."

"You ready?" The thin man seemed anxious to begin the proceedings.

"No," Marsh replied. "Does it make any difference?" He leaned forward and kissed the girl on her forehead. "I'll see you later—I promise. And if you think of anything original while you're waiting—do it."

"I can't watch," she took hold of his shirt.

"Yes you can—I need you up there—go on." Marsh pried loose her fingers and walked to the rusty iron door leading into the enclosure.

His captors moved to his side, the large man holding the gun centered at Marsh's crotch. Marsh smiled at him. "One day I'm going to make you wish you'd never tried this," he said. "And don't forget, if you're too slow with that antivenin, you've blown your own game."

Jammed with windblown sand, the bolt on the door was stuck in its socket. Marsh waited until the tall skinny American was completely occupied with it, then spun round.

Pushing the muzzle of the gun sideways with one hand, he sank his fist into the stomach of its owner bringing his knee up fiercely as the large man folded. He had the satisfaction of feeling bone slam into his hard thigh muscle before he was struck agonizingly in the ribs by a length of wood swung expertly in the hands of the man who was clever with a knife.

Seconds later, gasping in pain he was thrust headlong through the door.

The enclosure appeared smaller from the inside. Constructed from sheets of old corrugated iron nailed to gnarled wooden posts, it was ten feet high and solid enough to contain several determined men.

Leaning weakly with his back to the door, Marsh watched the spectators gather on the crude framework bordering one edge of the box in which he was imprisoned. The large man was bleeding from the nose.

"Steven—" The Israeli girl seemed so close yet so far away. She had nothing but his name to say.

"The drawings, Marsh. Your last chance." The injured American spoke through a handkerchief, dabbing at his face.

Pushing the pain in his side away, Marsh stripped off his shirt and held it loosely by the collar with his left hand. In his hand he held the knife. A futile fight which could end only in pain—he wondered how bad it was going to be.

One of the men was lifting a thin plank to reveal a narrow hole at ground level on the far side of the enclosure. It had begun.

The rattlesnake was larger than any Marsh had seen in photographs.

A red diamondback over six feet long emerged gracefully to join the man trapped in the steel box. It seemed unwilling to leave the boundary, moving slowly along one side, its head only a few inches from the ground.

Marsh possessed one slender advantage over other men who could have had the misfortune to find themselves in his position—he was not afraid of snakes.

Ten feet away from him, one of nature's more deadly machines had suddenly become aware of his presence, but to Steven Marsh it was nothing more than a reptile capable of killing him with one single strike of its fangs. The horror and revulsion experienced by many people when confronted by a venomous snake was mercifully wholly absent. The advantage, Marsh thought, was not going to be of much bloody use.

It slithered towards him, its head rising slightly as it approached. He stood absolutely still, knowing it would be a one-sided fight, if there was going to be time to fight at all.

"Changed your mind, Marsh?" On the balcony, the thin man threw a handful of sand at the snake. Immediately, the rattle started. Marsh counted eight segments on the tail.

Not yet fully aroused, the diamondback was now no more than three feet away from him, its head not yet in the classic striking position.

Inadvertently Marsh moved the shirt and the rattle became louder.

Toxic effects on the central nervous system, destruction of the walls of blood vessels and profuse bleeding caused by the retardation of coagulation—just some of the results of snake bite he could remember. Unless they got the antivenin into him quickly, one good strike from a bastard this big would inject enough venom to kill him in a few seconds. And then later—if he survived—they'd put him in here again for a second time with the pain fresh in his mind. Marsh thought that if it was the last thing he ever did he would have to avoid a repetition of this.

Gripping the knife, he prepared for a sideways swipe at its head if it attempted a strike at the dangling shirt. Maybe he could get its fangs tangled in it long enough to slice through its throat.

So quickly he could hardly believe it had moved, the head darted forwards. There was a fearful view of curved fangs and gaping throat and the snake was back in its waiting position. Incredibly, Marsh had not even had time to consider using his knife let alone begin moving it.

Gradually, he moved the shirt away from his body until his arm was almost horizontal. Then he flicked the material.

This time the knife whistled six inches away from the slender neck as it shot forward, Marsh struggling not to move his legs in order to avoid distracting the snake's attention from the shirt. His effort failed, the huge brown and white coils reforming to bring the blunt nose of the head to face him.

Frightened, not because it was a snake but because of the awful efficiency of the reptile confronting him, he strained every nerve and muscle until his body ached with tension.

It was going to strike him high up on his left thigh and no man could be quick enough. The noise from its rattle filled his head and sweat was pouring into his eyes. Now—no wait. Use the side of the knife—cut upwards as the head flew towards him.

A sudden noise from the spectators filtered through the continuous rattle. Shouting, and a curious gasping.

Desperately trying not to lose his concentration, he prepared himself for the strike.

A figure flew through the air to land heavily just behind the body of the snake.

Marsh sprang sideways, the open mouth grazing the side of his knee. No time for the knife—no time for anything but the critical need to make his sluggish body escape from the wicked fangs of the animal trying to kill him.

From a heap on the sand the thin man was struggling wildly to his feet. Sheer, unadulterated terror showed in every feature of his face.

Foolishly he waved his arms and started shouting in a high-pitched lisp. Simultaneously the other American fired three shots at the snake.

Inside the corrugated iron arena the noise of the gunshots was tremendous.

Injured by one of the bullets and now thoroughly enraged, the diamondback transformed itself from a coolly calculating reptile into a frantic six-foot length of venomous death.

Slithering from one side of the box to the other, it struck viciously at anything which moved, spraying venom on the steel walls. Safe for half a second, Marsh glanced upwards to see the large man fire twice more in an attempt to kill the snake. Of the girl there was no sign.

Marsh made up his mind. Thrusting himself off one wall, in three bounds he was across the enclosure and hurling himself upwards. Pivoting on the raw edge of the sheet iron on his unprotected stomach, he swung his legs back, grabbed hold of the top and flung himself over.

Five feet from the ground, something had struck the heel of his left shoe but incredibly he was safe. Instantly there was a long scream from behind him followed by a fusillade of gunshots.

From nowhere the girl appeared to join him.

Bleeding from a deep cut across his stomach and with nasty wounds in both hands, Marsh wasted no time.

"Run," he yelled. "Keep in front of me."

Suspecting that the large man had exhausted his ammunition in an attempt to save his colleague from the snake—an attempt which, by the scream he had heard, sounded as though it had been unsuccessful, Marsh was still not prepared to take a chance. They would gun down the girl without compunction but, with his secret intact, Marsh knew he was relatively safe from a fatal shot in the back.

Skirting scrubby outcrops of sagebrush, Sharmila was running like a gazelle across the desert. Marsh let her lead him a half mile from the derelict house before shouting at her to stop. No shots had followed their escape.

She turned round to see him literally smothered in blood.

"Oh my God," she gasped.

Marsh managed a smile. Pumping out of him as he ran, blood from the gashes caused by the sharp edge of the steel had turned his hands and waist to red.

She produced a small handkerchief, returned it to her pocket, then stripped off her sweater using it to swab away the worst of the blood. After inspecting the wounds, she made ready to throw away the stained garment.

"No," Marsh panted. "You look real good without it but put it back on. A couple of hours from now and you're going to need it." He glanced upwards at the sun. "One of us better keep covered up and my shirt's back there somewhere."

"Apart from those are you all right?" She pointed to his cuts.

"If you mean am I suffering from shock or snake bite the answer's no—what happened?"

"I couldn't stand it any longer," she said seriously. "So I made him think I was going to get back on the ground. When he tried to stop me I pushed him in."

Marsh shook his head in wonder. "Just like that."

"What do you mean?" She pulled the bloodstained sweater over her head, tugging her long hair loose from the polo neck.

"Nothing," Marsh said, "nothing at all, but thanks. I had a definite feeling that you were just in time. You're a very surprising person."

"As well as being a real one?"

"Very real, Sharmila. Now climb up on my shoulders a minute and have a look to see what our friends are doing." He crouched down hoping the strain of lifting her wouldn't re-start the bleeding.

When he lowered her again she touched the old scar

on his chest. "You're going to have two now," she said. "I can't see anything but juniper trees and sagebrush. You decide."

In order to formulate even the simplest of plans, Marsh knew he would have to take a calculated guess on what had happened after he had escaped from the steel corral. Had the thin man received a bite from the rattler? Would the other American follow them on foot? He considered his own position for a moment.

"Seeing as how we don't know where we are there's only one thing we can do," he said. "Pretty soon it's going to be too damn hot to do anything and I haven't got a shirt. That can be serious out here—we haven't any water either."

"And I haven't got any shoes, Steven—I can't walk on hot sand; I know, I've tried it in Israel."

Marsh remembered how she'd run out to her car at the motel, leaving her sandals inside the door. "We're not very well equipped between us, are we?" he said. "Maybe both of us are lousy at our jobs."

She smiled at him. "You've got the real drawings and I've still got you—we can't be that bad."

Marsh took her hand. "Come on, brown eyes, we've got to find a road and make sure those snake charmers don't catch up with us."

He squinted at the rising sun, no longer a red ball but a dazzling white area of sky already radiating enough heat to make him wish he could have a drink.

Striking off northwards, two very different people began to walk slowly into one of Nevada's wilder places, both of them grateful for the company of the other and both of them still numb from the events which had overtaken them so suddenly six hours before. The second part of their ordeal had only just begun.

CHAPTER SIX

Northwest of California's Death Valley, just across the border into the state of Nevada, the Las Vegas bombing and gunnery range had been preserved carefully by the American Military. An area of splendid desert wilderness, travel on any of the tracks leading into it is strictly prohibited unless previously authorized. Applications to enter the range are rarely granted.

Because of infrequent use it is customary for an aerial survey of the range to be made before any high explosives are detonated in any section of it and, although inspections of this kind are generally acknowledged to be a complete waste of time by the U.S. Air Force, they are carried out as thoroughly as time permits.

Pilots assigned to the job are accustomed to scanning the surface for wheel tracks or even the odd car which may for some obscure reason have ventured off the main highway, but the task is a boring one and the low incidence of sightings does nothing to enliven it.

This morning, a rising heat haze was distorting the distant view of Quartzite mountain, its top reaching nearly eight thousand feet above sea level into a pale blue sky. James Rivel took one last look at it, banked his survey aircraft, and began the search pattern he was supposed to be following. Ahead of him through the windshield, the mesa lying between Tolicha peak and Black Mountain obscured the delicate pattern on the floor of Gold Flat which he had been able to watch before changing course.

To his left, winding like a black pencil line over the smooth texture of the desert, highway 95 became progressively thinner and thinner until it disappeared far to the north into a glassy blending of sand and sky. A vast area of shimmering nothing and an area in which nothing moved at this time of day.

Rivel let his attention wander for a second. Then he saw the wheel marks.

From Death Valley, a minor road cutting through Grapevine Canyon meets highway 95 at a point adjacent to the western edge of the range. Many years ago the road had continued onwards as a track leading to an old house now derelict and located some way inside the boundary. Today, from the air, the track was a different color and Rivel knew what that meant.

He pushed the stick forward to reduce altitude and buzzed the building, wondering if any visitors were still around. There was no sign of the car that had been here and he considered it unlikely that the place had been used for more than one or two nights for some unknown or possibly illegal purpose. Kids perhaps or some stupid bastard hiding out.

Flicking the transmit switch on his radio he reported his findings then continued flying northwards, his curiosity mildly aroused by his discovery.

Three minutes later he saw the people. Two dots moving slowly between the faded green patches of sagebrush.

This time the lieutenant in flight control sounded much more interested.

"Of course I'm sure," Rivel said. "I've seen people before—I even saw one that looked like you before I got in this goddam aircraft this morning. You are a people, aren't you?"

"Two?" the lieutenant inquired patiently. "You said two?"

"Yeah. That's one more than one and one less than three, I think." Rivel turned the plane, stood it on its wing tip and saw them wave to him.

"They're waving," he said into the microphone. "Probably recognize me. You'd better send someone out before the heat gets them. They're heading for the highway but if they started from the old house they've had quite a walk already."

The pilot listened to the reply from Flight Control. "No," he said, "a car'll do it. By the time you get here you should be able to see them." He grinned. "No —definitely not two girls in bikinis otherwise I wouldn't have radioed. I'm carrying on with the survey—I'll see you at four o'clock."

If James Rivel had known why these two people should have been walking out on the range he would undoubtedly have been more interested. But he was not an imaginative man, and the pleasant contemplation of the firm promise received from the girl he had met in Reno last week soon provided diversion enough from the task of inspecting the desert floor.

A thousand feet below Steven Marsh and Sharmila Talmai met the arrival of the aircraft with a mixture of relief and apprehension.

Two hours had elapsed since they had started walking. Two hours in which they had learned to hate the heat and curse the sand beneath their feet. Although still some way from its zenith the sun was nevertheless extremely hot and the air had long since lost the clear freshness of early morning.

Marsh had not fared well. The back of his neck and his shoulders were a livid red and his feet were raw and blistered. Out of plain necessity he had given his socks to Sharmila to protect her feet from sand already too hot to be bearable and he had been walking with shoes filled with abrasive sand for nearly half an hour.

Both of them were dehydrated, very thirsty and suffering from a dryness in the mouth which seemed to become worse with each step.

Unsure whether they would be pursued or not, Marsh had struck a northwards route, deliberately avoiding heading back towards the unseen road by which they had been brought into the desert until he was sure that no one was following them. For the entire journey he had been thinking of what they should do once they hit the highway.

Their point of emergence from the desert could well have been roughly predicted by the two Americans and neither Marsh nor the girl were in any condition for a further confrontation or roadside scuffle. Whether or not there would be sufficient traffic to prevent anything like that from taking place remained to be seen, for he still had no definite idea of where they were or how far from the nearest town they might be.

Since their escape, their conversation had quite literally dried up and, for the last hour, they had trudged along almost in complete silence.

Marsh managed to summon a few drops of saliva to moisten his cracked lips. "I hope you're right about that plane," he said. "I mean about it belonging to the United States Air Force. I'd hate to think we'd waved to someone who was deliberately trying to track us down."

Sharmila stepped round a withered clump of sagebrush and stopped walking to answer him. "Maybe the Air Force was trying to find us," she said. "They might have been."

Marsh shook his head. "They don't even know who we are and they certainly didn't know we were lost. That plane saw us by accident—I hope."

He looked at her puffed cheeks, scarlet with sunburn and thought that he owed a lot to her for what she'd done, even though it was her fault they were here at all.

"We'll reach the road soon," he said. "It can't be far away unless it's made a right-angled turn somewhere and roads in this part of the world don't do that."

Marsh was right. Fifteen minutes later they were standing on the asphalt strip that was highway 95. If necessary both of them were ready to return to the desert or fight beside the road if the wrong car appeared.

Having timed it to a nicety, the driver of car 14 of the Nevada highway patrol had no difficulty in recognizing the two people he had been diverted to collect.

White sweater caked in dried blood where she had used it on Marsh's wounds, at first sight the Israeli girl appeared to be terribly injured whilst Marsh himself looked like something out of a horror movie where his cuts had been weeping.

"Jesus," the driver remarked to his companion as they drew up on the shoulder of the road. "They should've sent the bloodwagon. I don't feel like cleaning up after this lot." He loosened the strap on his holster and opened the door, standing behind it to inspect Marsh more closely.

"If you haven't brought any water we'll catch a lift with someone else thanks," Marsh croaked.

The officer reached into the car and produced a canteen which he handed over without saying anything. Marsh passed it directly to Sharmila.

"I suppose you were asked to meet us?" Marsh asked when he had taken a drink.

"How bad are you hurt," the patrolman ignored the question.

"Mostly sunburn," Marsh told him. "The cuts aren't too bad—just look a mess. She's okay, too," he nodded at Sharmila. "That's just blood from my scratches."

"Can you both make it back to Vegas in the car?" the driver asked. "We'll get you fixed up there."

"Thanks," Marsh said. He went to the rear door and helped Sharmila to collapse gratefully on the seat.

"All I want is a cold shower and a gallon of suncream," she said. "It gets hotter than I thought it would out here."

The driver waited for a truck to lumber by then

turned the car before heading back down the highway towards his headquarters in Las Vegas.

Twisting round in his seat the other officer produced a notebook. "Save time if you do some explaining on the way," he said. "What were you doing out there on the range?"

"What?" Marsh said.

"People just don't arrive in the middle of the Nevada bombing range without a shirt on. And they never have pretty girls with them, especially barefoot girls covered in blood."

Marsh thought furiously. There was only one way and, although it might easily prove the wrong thing to do, no explanation was going to satisfy the local police no matter how ingenious he made it.

"We didn't know it was a bombing range," Sharmila said. "We'd have kept to the road if we had."

Marsh gripped her leg to stop her. "It's okay," he said to the patrolman, "I'm sorry about this." He reached into his hip pocket and slipped out a thin plastic wallet. "You'd better check these out on your radio unless you'd rather wait until you get back."

The officer inspected the two security cards he had been given, handing them to the driver when he had finished. Then he turned round again.

"How about an off-the-record story, Mr. Marsh," he said, "otherwise I'll never sleep trying to figure out what the hell has been going on up here."

"We've been doing some basic research on rattle-snakes," Marsh grinned. "I found a real good one ear-lier today. You can have the whole story for a ciga-rette."

"Keep the packet," the officer said, "and I guess you might as well keep the story for all the good it'd do me. I suppose the girl's with you?"

"No—he's with me," Sharmila said. "Thank you for picking us up though, I really couldn't have walked any further." She smiled and used her eyes. "No, I mean that—we're both very grateful—really."

"Okay," the patrolman waved the wallet. "I'd better hold on to this until I get it cleared. Maybe one day I'll have a job where fairy tales are only stories you read in books. You want some more water?" He looked at Sharmila.

She shook her head. "Not yet, thank you."

Marsh took the offered canteen and drank deeply, trying unsuccessfully to ignore the increasing pain across his shoulders. First he'd have to get the sunburn fixed up and then he'd start thinking about what to say to Dahl. He lay back uncomfortably, turning his head to address the girl beside him.

"Suppose we stop working for a while?" he said. "Seeing as how we're not very good at it."

"Is that the only reason?" she asked.

"No, I hurt too much to keep on worrying about you."

"I'm all right, Steven," she reassured him.

"I don't mean that. I want to stop thinking you're trying to swing a deal—just for the next day or two."

She smiled at him. "You'll help me with the CIA?"

"I figure we better help each other." Marsh winked at her.

"Then we've temporarily retired," she said, reaching for the water. "I'll drink to that."

And somehow or other, Marsh thought, before long I have to decide what to do about you, Miss Talmai. He closed his eyes, sick to death with a job that allowed a man no time to be himself and tired, so tired, of having to think three jumps ahead. Beside him, the young Israeli girl was thinking very much the same thing.

Warren Dahl chewed angrily on his cold cigar and made a further series of deep indentations in his blotter with the sharp end of his ball-point pen. Three days had gone by since his department had bungled the job of recovering the Israeli drawings; three days during which his phone had driven him to the point where he had finally exploded in front of the young White House executive who had flown all the way from Washington to make an inquiry. And that had only made matters worse, he thought bitterly. Shouting at Government officials was not calculated to improve his image let alone solve the problem.

He drew a circle around the dots on his blotter and pushed a button on his intercom. "Okay, Jean," he said, "show them in—both together."

Marsh held the door for Sharmila to enter the room ahead of him.

"Hello, Dahl," he said. "I didn't expect to see you again so soon. This is Miss Talmai, Miss Sharmila Talmai. She's a friend of mine."

Dahl wondered if Marsh knew what he'd got hold of. "I understand you're on vacation in the States, Miss Talmai?" he said dryly. "I would have thought someone from Israel would have known better than to go walking around in the desert." He stood up and carried a chair from the corner of the room. "You'd better sit down—they told me you've both got sore feet."

Marsh lit a cigarette and blew a thin stream of smoke into the air-conditioning vent. "Why send a car to bring us all the way here to San Francisco?" he said. "The last time I spoke to you on the phone you didn't sound very interested in my minor problems."

"Marsh," Dahl said, "you give me a pain. You worry me, too. You're here, both of you, to answer my questions. The Government paid your hospital bill and I figure it's about time we had another talk. Now suppose you tell me what you were doing with this girl in Nevada."

Marsh raised his eyebrows. "I wasn't doing anything with her," he said. "I don't think you know how hot it is out there this time of year."

Dahl sighed and used his intercom again. Sharmila

stood up and walked to the door without being asked. "Have a nice talk," she said. "I'll wait outside."

"Okay," Marsh said, when she had left the room. "Now you listen to this, Dahl. I came over here to help you. I was told it was a joint British-American job. But oh no, the bloody CIA wanted the whole thing to themselves—well you can have it and when I get back I'll tell them in London what a helpful bastard you are. You were given the whole thing on a plate so don't start lecturing me—I can look after my end—you look after yours."

Warren Dahl thought Marsh might not have rehearsed this after all. He applied a flame to his cigar. "I suppose you don't know what happened?" he inquired, staring at the Englishman through a cloud of smoke.

"Don't tell me you blew it," Marsh said incredulously.

Dahl shook his head. "We got the helicopter and we got the drawings on the road to Carson City but someone must have heard something. There was a hell of a mess on highway 395. I told you about the bomb we found in the Firebird when I spoke to you on the phone."

Marsh sensed a trap. "What time did it go off," he said, with interest.

"It didn't." Dahl's eyes bored into him. "They had a machine-gun set up at an intersection. The Firebird and a Chevrolet drove right into it. The State Police got there about half an hour after it happened. Two guys in the Chev, the bastard with the gun and one of our best men—all dead. Like I said, a mess."

"And the drawings—" Marsh inquired.

Dahl reached into a drawer and withdrew a dirty briefcase. "The Police found it still in the Firebird— we were lucky. The drawings have already been flown out to Europe."

"So you've got a leak," Marsh said. "Someone here

knew about our idea of bringing that chopper down. The big bad CIA's got a rotten bit in it. You want to look out, Dahl—Washington might want another scapegoat."

The CIA man leaned forwards. "Never mind about Washington—screw Washington. What interests me is the bomb."

Marsh appeared mildly puzzled. "The whole thing's pretty interesting when you think about it," he said. "But at least it had a happy ending. I bet the State Police were real pleased about helping you out."

"The bomb," Dahl repeated. "The bomb. Whoever heard we were going to hit the chopper only found out late in the piece otherwise they could have changed their delivery time or flown the helicopter some place else. They only got on to it after we'd got the case. So a quick chase up the highway into a neat trap—a trap that bloody nearly worked."

"Ah," Marsh exclaimed, wondering if he should make the effort to jump to the conclusion Dahl was working up to. "And of course your bomb must have been planted before the Firebird left here."

Dahl smiled briefly. "We stole that car and repainted it the day before—just to make sure nothing could go wrong. Something stinks, Marsh, and I think it's you." He pointed a finger across his desk.

"Stop it," Marsh exclaimed in mock horror, "I can't stand it any longer. I confess. I planted the bomb, machine-gunned the Firebird and handed over the briefcase to the Police. It was me, Dahl—I did it all." He stood up and leaned forward. "And that's why you searched my room and left me in the desert to die!"

"Sit down," Dahl snarled. "Tell me about the desert."

Marsh told him.

At the end of it Warren Dahl was under the impression that for some inexplicable reason he had been told the truth but he had not the slightest intention of believing any of it.

"So the girl's here in the States to try and bust open these companies who're stealing Israel's secrets," he said at length, "and she thought you might have some inside information."

"I believe her," Marsh said reasonably, "so does someone else. That's why those characters who took us into the desert thought they'd be better off if we both suffered fatal snake bites. Whoever these twelve companies have got working for them are fairly nasty. I think it's about time we started pushing someone around ourselves but this is your country so I'm going to let you do it."

The description of Marsh's ordeal with the snake had quietened the CIA man and the fresh fang marks deep in the heel of his shoe seemed genuine enough. Later today he'd check out the old house in the Nevada gunnery range—that much at least should provide some evidence to substantiate what Marsh had said, but apart from questioning the girl there was little else he could do. The girl, he thought, would be word perfect. Dahl wondered how long Marsh would take to get her into bed.

"You're to stay in San Francisco," Dahl said. "I had this flown in from London in case you had other ideas." He handed Marsh an envelope.

It contained a single sheet of thin white paper bearing two paragraphs of coded instructions. The message was entirely clear to the Englishman. "Full official co-operation," Marsh said. "At your service, Mr. Dahl. What do I do first?" The unconcealed sarcasm in his voice had no visible effect on the CIA man.

"First," Dahl instructed, "you get the hell out of here while I talk to your girl friend. I'll call your hotel when I'm ready with some more questions. Give me your passport."

"It's back in the motel in Las Vegas," Marsh lied. "You'll have to get someone to pick it up for you. I'm not going anywhere." He waved his sheet of paper.

"That's what this says. Come and have a drink with me this evening."

Dahl opened the door for him. "I'll do you a favor," he said, "make sure you remember."

"You owe me one," Marsh told him. "What is it?"

"I'll book the girl into the same hotel."

Marsh grinned at him. "That way you can watch both of us with the same men. But thanks. If I think of anything interesting I'll call you."

Sharmila was talking to Dahl's secretary. She appeared relaxed and anxious to be of assistance. She smiled at Marsh.

Sure he was about to be conned, Dahl followed her back into his office. She had, he thought, the roundest bottom he had seen for some time.

CHAPTER SEVEN

Directly ahead of them the distant lights of Sacramento lit the skyline with a dull orange glare. Marsh switched off the car radio and picked up the map from the seat.

"Another hundred and thirty-nine miles," he said. "This is the third time in three days I've done this trip and it gets longer and longer."

There was no answer from the girl beside him.

"Stop sulking," he said, "I've already told you. If I hadn't wanted you to come with me I'd have left you back at the hotel."

"But it was easier this way, wasn't it?" she said angrily. "And you needed me to help you make fools out of Dahl's men."

"They don't need any help. Anyway, Dahl knew he couldn't stop me from leaving the hotel if I really wanted to. He thought I'd stay put because of the instructions I'd got from London."

"But clever Steven Marsh chooses to ignore his instructions," she said, "and here we are on the road to Reno in a Hertz car as though we're a couple of tourists. But I'm just along for the ride—right?"

"Wrong," Marsh replied. "You made me an offer and I haven't decided what to do about it yet so I still need you with me. And you've got the wrong idea about London, too. Not long ago you were telling me that Israel thought the British were acting only in their own interests—what makes you think anything's changed?"

She put her hands behind her head and stretched.

"You mean London said you were to carry on—I should've guessed."

"So should Dahl," Marsh grinned, "and if he tries to decode the message it still won't help him. Sometimes the Americans are pretty stupid. I've had instructions like that before but never countersigned by a certain gentleman in the Foreign Office."

"When are you going to decide?" she asked.

"About the MIG fuselage and the SCUD missile?"

"Yes."

"When I get to England."

This time she was furious. "But I've told you we will deal only with you, not your government." Her eyes flashed dangerously.

"I understand that, Sharmila."

"Then you must decide—it is important."

He glanced briefly at her. "You're really sure I've got something to trade?"

For a moment Marsh thought she was going to hit him. With obvious effort she forced herself to sit back in the seat, her usually generous mouth compressed into a tight line.

"You think it's a game, don't you," she said bitterly. "In Israel there are thousands of people who would give their lives just to gain a few more precious years of peace if what we have now can be called peace. And yet there are people like you—people who will never understand or even care."

Marsh thought that the Israeli dossier on him must have missed out a couple of important facts. He lit a cigarette and carried on threading the car through the late evening traffic, following the highway 40 route signs through the outskirts of Sacramento. By now Dahl would have set the West Coast CIA network into action and he could not afford to have the girl upset. They were by no means out of the woods yet.

"I've told you why we're going to Reno," he said quietly. "We're going to pick up the drawings, collect my passport, collect your passport and then we're getting out of here. It won't be long before Dahl finds out he got hold of the wrong drawings and then all hell will break loose. If we're still in the States we'll never get out. Even this way it's not going to be easy."

"And you won't decide until you get to England?"

"You're coming with me," Marsh said.

"What for?"

"Because our friends with the snake are probably looking for you. Because the CIA are definitely looking for you and because I might want to make a deal with you."

"I can look after myself." She was using the same efficient voice she'd used at the motel when Marsh had first met her. "We have many real friends in the States."

Friends, Marsh thought. In this business the word had a different meaning altogether. One day there would be time to climb into a car somewhere, anywhere, with a real friend and just drive without having to wonder what lay ahead. He wished this attractive Jewish girl had never appeared on the scene to complicate things.

"I hate you," she said flatly, "and I've known you've had the Kfir drawings all along."

With Sacramento behind him but with many, long, frustrating miles still to go, Marsh settled into his seat as comfortably as his sunburn would allow and tried to convince himself that she was nothing more than a trained MOSSAD operator, committed to her assignment and her country as he was to his. For some reason the fact she was a young woman was making a difference, yet Marsh knew there was more to it than that. He looked at her again casually, unable to determine what was bothering him.

She switched on the radio. "Sometimes I wish it was different," she said, echoing his own thoughts. "One day perhaps."

Marsh said nothing, watching the road endlessly unfurl itself beneath the beams of the headlights. For a long while he thought of nothing at all.

Three hours later he reached across and shook her gently by the shoulder. She muttered something in her sleep then woke with a start.

"We're here," Marsh said. "We'll get your passport first and the money you mentioned. Where do we go?"

"Carry on straight into Reno," she replied sleepily.

"There's one small problem," Marsh said. "How do I know you won't try to be funny and persuade your friend to pull a gun on me now you know I can take you to the drawings?"

"You don't," she said shortly. "Down there"—she pointed suddenly to a wide boulevard leading off to the left. "Take the next turning to the right and it's the second house down."

The wizened old Jewess who opened the door seemed nervous.

Sitting in the car ready for trouble, Marsh was unable to hear what Sharmila was saying. Something told him all was not well.

He wound down the window and shouted at her. "Leave it, Sharmila."

She turned and shook her head. "It's okay, just wait a moment."

Carrying a small suitcase the old lady reappeared to stand silhouetted in the dimly lit doorway. Marsh heard the name Max mentioned several times then Sharmila was running back towards him down the path.

He had the door opened and the car rolling before she reached it.

"Move," she instructed breathlessly, "there's something wrong."

"I'll tell you when to turn."

Marsh gunned the motor making the tires squeal.

"Turn left," she shouted suddenly. "Sorry, I wasn't thinking." She swiveled round to check behind.

"Just tell me which way," Marsh said. "I'll watch out for a tail. What happened?"

"There are traffic lights about four blocks away. Go straight across and we should meet 395. Nothing happened—or all the wrong things happened. The old lady is arthritic. I've never seen her on her feet before. A friend of mine—Max Navon—looks after her; I think she's his grandmother. She wouldn't say where he was. I just got the creeps—Max should've been there. She wouldn't tell me anything."

"You mean you had a feeling?" Marsh said.

"Mmm. You know what I mean."

"I know. I hope you're wrong though. Better check your things."

She rummaged in the case, producing a soiled passport and a thick envelope. "There are about nine hundred dollars left. Is that enough?"

"Plenty. All we have to do now is make sure no one stops us. It's all clear behind. Maybe you were wrong." Marsh applied the brakes swearing at the red light ahead.

"The old lady was scared—I could smell it."

"But she handed over your case. I take it Max is one of Israel's closer friends? Does he work for MOSSAD?" She gave him the envelope.

"No, but he's helped me a lot. I was given a list of people living in the States whom I could contact—Max is one of them."

The lights changed. Still no car had appeared in his driving mirror and Marsh began to believe they had both imagined trouble when none existed. If he had stretched his imagination a little further the simplicity of the trap would have become painfully clear, but he was concerned with his driving and for the moment the obvious did not occur to him.

Only when he stopped at the wire gate leading to the tiny airfield twenty minutes later did the first suspicion cross his mind.

Grabbing Sharmila's suitcase he ripped it open and tipped the contents out on to the floor. A neat incision in the lining of the lid told him what he wanted to know.

Wrenching open the door, he threw the case on to the road and ground the bug to pieces under his heel.

"You and your bloody friends," he shouted. "Get over there to the building—run. I won't be a minute."

Sensibly not stopping to discover what had prompted Marsh to yell at her, Sharmila had hardly time to leave the car before he began to savagely realign it sideways across the gateway. Locking all the doors behind him he paused long enough to smash the top of the distributor with a rock, then he too was running towards the single low building at the end of the airstrip.

His original plan might still work but only if things went smoothly during the next few minutes. If they didn't he would have no choice but to get tough—even then there might not be time.

Sharmila was waiting for him at the door.

"Transmitter planted in your case," he explained. "We probably haven't got long. Be specially nice to the guy in here." He pushed open the glass door and walked inside hoping the man on night duty would be the one he had met before.

It was.

"Wish I had a job like yours," Marsh said pleasantly. "Remember me?"

A stocky, fresh-faced man dressed in dirty jeans and a short-sleeved shirt removed his feet unhurriedly from the desk and folded his newspaper.

"Oh, it's you," he said. "Come for your stuff?" He examined Sharmila with evident interest.

Marsh nodded. "Sorry I left it here so long."

"I'll get it." He went to a derelict filing cabinet, lifted off the top and reached inside.

"It was just a parcel with my photos," Marsh said,

wishing he could think of some way to accelerate matters.

"Got it." The stocky man handed him a brown paper package whilst studying each curve of Sharmila as though unable to believe his good fortune in having such an attractive visitor in his office.

Marsh dropped a twenty-dollar note in between the dirty coffee cups littering the desk. "I've got another job," he said. "More aerial photography, but not a forest fire this time—city lights."

"You want to rent a plane again?"

"Right—going to take a friend with me on this one," Marsh winked at him.

"Some job—how long do you want it for?"

"Not more than three or four hours." Marsh produced a wad of notes from his hip pocket. "Same rates as before?" He peeled off three hundred dollars.

The one-man airline operator shrugged. "If you want to spend your nights flying around the desert I'll be glad to take your money, mister."

"We're in a hurry," Sharmila said sweetly.

"Only got the Cessna 150 but you're only cleared for singles anyway, aren't you?"

Marsh nodded. "The Cessna's fine—how's the fuel?"

"Full. Here, sign this, I'll fill in the rest—still got your first form here somewhere—I can get the details off that." He picked up the money. "I guess your kind of photography must pay well."

"Can we leave now?" Sharmila asked. "It's late already." She inclined her head slightly. Through the window a pair of headlights had stopped at the fence line outside the gate.

"You want me to help you start it?" The owner of the Cessna seemed torn between accompanying Sharmila as far as possible and returning to his newspaper.

"I can manage," Marsh told him. "Maybe I could mention your airline if the photos turn out well." He turned to leave. "We'll be back later. Thanks."

Sharmila smiled her appreciation, walking from the office with the knowledge that she was being mentally undressed for the tenth time in as many minutes.

Outside Marsh grabbed her hand and began running towards the red and white aircraft parked outside on the grass. Shortly before they reached it, a series of loud crashes indicated that someone had lost their temper at the gate. Simultaneously, the rudimentary runway lights were switched on.

He leaped into the cockpit and began flicking switches, praying nothing would go wrong. Beside him Sharmila was buckling her seat belt.

The motor fired, coughed and stopped. Marsh started swearing, knowing there could only be seconds left now.

On the third attempt the 100 horsepower Continental burst noisily into life. He opened the throttle, checked his controls as the plane began to move then swung its nose to point between the narrow row of lights.

The Cessna had accelerated for less than fifty feet before two unnerving events took place. A bullet zipped through the sheet metal canopy behind them and the runway lights were abruptly extinguished. Seconds later, headlights which had previously remained stationary at the airfield gate flickered through the side window as a car came tearing across the grass towards them. From the course it was taking there was no mistaking the driver's intentions.

"Hang on," Marsh shouted over the roar of the engine, "and keep your head down."

But the driver of the car had underestimated the acceleration of such a light aircraft, the headlights dropping behind as the Cessna picked up vital speed. No more bullets punctured the cockpit but Marsh knew there were plenty of other vulnerable areas which, once they were in the air, were as critical to their survival as their own fragile bodies.

For a while the car headlights had provided sufficient

illumination to enable him to keep the Cessna on course but now, still not yet airborne, there was nothing ahead of him but total blackness.

Three days ago he had flown the same plane off this strip in late afternoon and the memory of the chain link wire fence surrounding the airfield was making him sweat.

Now, Marsh thought, now before the undercarriage catches the fence to turn us into a cartwheel of flaming wreckage. He eased the stick back, feeling the wheels start to leave the ground in a series of gentle bumps.

The Cessna skipped once, lurched upwards and suddenly was airborne, its tires skimming over the invisible fence with only inches to spare. Marsh put it into the steepest climb he dared attempt, trying to remember if there were any trees nearby.

"You okay?" he shouted above the engine roar to Sharmila.

"Tell you in a minute when I'm sure we're off the ground."

Breathing more easily now they had gained precious altitude, he checked his instruments noting that the fuel gauge showed full. Twenty-six U.S. gallons, enough to take them 560 miles if they were lucky. And if they were unlucky, that was not going to be anything like as far as Marsh wanted to go.

A few minutes later when the engine noise seemed more familiar and Marsh had trimmed the aircraft, Sharmila reached behind her to plug one of the bullet holes with a screwed up handkerchief.

"Next time I'll fly out of L.A. on a Jumbo, thanks," she said.

"If you'd tried that this time Dahl would've picked you up before you even reached the departure lounge," Marsh told her. "This way's more fun."

"It was my fault again, wasn't it?" she said.

"Probably, but we needed the money. Maybe Max isn't so friendly after all."

"No, it wasn't that. I know what happened. Those men who took us into the desert told you they'd been watching me, didn't they. They must have known about Max and guessed I'd go back there. I've only ever been to the house twice though—most of the time I was in San Francisco or Vegas."

"The opposition's a hell of a lot better organized than the CIA," Marsh said, "and I don't like the way they're clever with their electronics. First they plant a transmitter in my motel room which I didn't even look for, then they fix a bug in your suitcase and I didn't think of that either. I'm beginning to wonder if I get paid too much and I don't often feel that way."

"If you knew how difficult it must have been to get those Kfir missile drawings out of Israel you'd have an idea of how organized they are." She pulled her hair away from her face. "You're a funny man—things seem to work out for you, but only just and you don't give a damn, do you? You even left the drawings with that man at the airfield."

Marsh smiled to himself. "You've forgotten I was doing pretty well until you came along," he said. "I wouldn't say you've brought me good luck, would you?"

"I wasn't supposed to. I just wanted the drawings."

He picked up the parcel from the floor and placed it on her lap. "With my compliments," he said. "All you have to do is take them and jump out. Leave me my passport though, it's in there with them."

"I'll run off with the drawings when we get to Canada," she promised. "I'm too tired to jump."

Marsh lit a cigarette. "If we get to Canada," he said. "I have a nasty feeling my original escape plan isn't going to work now."

"But once we're over the Canadian border the CIA can't legally stop us from getting on a plane to Europe," she said.

"I was banking on the CIA not even knowing we'd

left the States," Marsh replied. "If that guy back at the strip's still in one piece he'll know we haven't rented his plane to take photos by now. I'll bet you that case of drawings Dahl will know inside a couple of hours. And never mind about him legally stopping us—the CIA doesn't work like that. You know as well as I do they can stop us stone dead anywhere in the world if they can find us—and I mean dead."

"How long will it take us, Steven?"

"To run out of gas or to cross the border?"

"To reach Canada."

Marsh did a quick calculation. "With no wind and holding our speed down for good economy—about four and three quarter hours."

"And how long to run out of fuel?"

"About the same time," Marsh said. "Like I said, it's more fun this way." He avoided mentioning his real fear of what could happen before the Cessna reached Canada. He also believed the girl was equally aware of the problem. By mutual consent, Marsh thought, we'll both pretend to worry about Dahl and our fuel instead.

Below them now, the carpet of glow-worms which was the outskirts of Reno was already falling behind, only the occasional light from a lonely house far out of town twinkling up out of the darkness.

A solitary car was traveling with them two thousand feet beneath the Cessna, reminding Marsh of his flight of three nights ago. Then he had been the hunter. Tonight things were very different.

CHAPTER EIGHT

Shortly after crossing the Oregon state boundary the trouble started. Flying almost entirely by instruments, Marsh had intentionally kept his radio open since leaving Reno half expecting to receive some sort of instructions from West Coast Air Traffic Control. When the communication finally came, Marsh knew they must have been tracking the aircraft for some time.

"Calling Cessna 150, 34 Sierra are you receiving, over." The reception was perfectly free of static sounding as though the transmitting station was remarkably close by.

"That's us," Marsh remarked. "I suppose it hasn't taken them long really."

"We're N 8534 S," Sharmila said. "It's on the wing."

"All American aircraft have the N," Marsh said. "They only use the last two numbers and the last letter for a call sign. They're calling us all right. I wonder if they do actually have us on radar?"

"34 Sierra please acknowledge. Repeat 34 Sierra."

"Get lost," Marsh said. "If you're expecting us to acknowledge you've got rocks in your head."

"Aren't you going to answer?" Sharmila asked.

"Not yet. They can't be sure they've got the right plane."

"How high are we flying now?"

"About nine thousand feet." He pointed to the glowing instrument panel.

"Well let's get down, we should be able to sneak in under the radar in a plane this small, shouldn't we?"

Marsh inspected his altimeter more closely. "I will in a minute. If they've got us spotted already they'll know it's us for sure if I start diving straight away. Relax there's plenty of time to try and slip out of their picture."

The operator in Air Traffic Control had no intention of giving up. At five minute intervals for the next twenty minutes Marsh was asked alternately to identify himself or acknowledge the call sign. On the fifth attempt the message was changed to one of a more personal and direct nature.

"Mr. Marsh, the United States Government requires and directs you to land at Salem or Portland. In accordance with international flight regulations you may not proceed beyond the Oregon-Washington state border unless you receive official clearance to do so."

Marsh shook his head. "We'll have to try and be clever," he said to Sharmila. "Otherwise they'll think of something nasty. Dahl will have made some phone calls by now and they're not going to let us fly to Canada if they can help it."

He put the Cessna into a shallow dive turning slightly to the west as if to give the impression he was heading for Portland still many miles to the north of them.

"Have you ever tried hedge-hopping in a light plane at night?" he inquired.

Sharmila smiled at him. "You don't have to explain," she said. "You fly the plane and I'll sit here and bite my nails."

"Never mind the fingernails—pray." He patted the parcel on her lap. "How about tearing those drawings into little bits and chucking them out the door? Then we could land at Portland and have a holiday."

"And no one would know if I'd done my job and no one would know if you'd done yours. It wouldn't work, Steven."

"But it'd be a hell of a lot better than flying into the side of a mountain."

"We won't," she assured him. "I may not have brought you good luck but we've still managed more or less. The mountains will move for us—you'll see."

Half an hour later, eyes aching with the strain, he began to believe she might be right.

Bright moonlight provided nothing more than a tantalizing and indistinct view of the terrain now less than a hundred feet below. Long dark shadows distorted what little Marsh could discern of the shallow hills and rolling countryside they were skimming over. Gradually he had eased the aircraft lower and lower until he knew it would be sheer suicide to reduce their height any further. Traveling at a speed of a hundred and twenty miles an hour, with visibility for major land masses of what he judged to be about a mile and a half, there was no great problem in avoiding hills, but twice already he had mistaken large dark areas for mountains. Realizing what had happened he had immediately reduced altitude only to find himself flying into a blind canyon or a moonlit prairie surrounded by tall pine trees. Total concentration was barely enough and Marsh knew that to continue relying on a precarious balance of luck and reflexes was more than foolhardy—it was madness. But still he carried on waiting for some indication that their ploy had worked.

Gradually changing course back to a more northerly direction in order to pass east of Portland, the tiny Cessna crept by Mount Jefferson and then on past the mighty snow covered cone of Mount Hood, Marsh slowly being forced to gain height again as they began to climb above the ragged tops of the Washington Cascade mountain chain.

Soon the ground became inhospitable in the extreme, cruel granite peaks eerie in the moonlight stretching ahead and to each side of them as far as they could see.

The sinister quality of the landscape had quietened Sharmila and her earlier optimism seemed to have evaporated.

"I didn't know you could fly like this," she said quietly, "you're a very surprising person."

And I didn't know either, Marsh thought grimly, screwing his eyes shut for half a second to clear the tears. Why hadn't traffic control tried again on the radio? In another half an hour Seattle would be behind them and, providing their fuel held out, Canada would not be far away. Surely Dahl wouldn't wait that long?

Dwarfed by the vastness of the Cascades, the red and white aircraft flew on through the night heading towards the huge pale mountain dominating the sky to the north.

"About ninety miles south-east of Seattle," Marsh announced. "That's Mount Rainier, all fourteen and a half thousand feet of it. I'm on home ground now—been here before."

"What about those others?" Sharmila asked. "The three we passed just after the Columbia river. The ones in a triangle."

"St. Helens, Mount Adams and the little one was Lemel, I think," Marsh said. "My geography's pretty lousy I'm afraid, even though I've worked in Washington a couple of times and I've flown over the Cascades before. In a proper aircraft though—not a toy like this."

"We're going to make it, aren't we?" she said.

Marsh grunted, not wishing to commit himself and not even wanting to decide yet whether to land brazenly at Vancouver or put the Cessna down somewhere less conspicuous. If by any stroke of good fortune their attempt to elude the American radar had been successful then Sharmila could perhaps be right, but he doubted if they'd be let off the hook so easily. Once in Canada Marsh could use his own authority or call on London for assistance—everything depended on how annoyed the CIA were and if they were prepared to risk a minor international scandal by trying something which with any luck might fail.

Having managed to get this far he was inclined to believe his earlier fears had been based on the bad luck which had been dogging him lately. Maybe the opposition who had so very nearly caught up with them in Reno had abandoned the project for the time being. After all, trying to trace the whereabouts of one insignificant Cessna somewhere inside a circle over a thousand miles in diameter called for an organization bigger even than they could possess.

Skirting well to the east of Rainier he lit his last but one cigarette and checked the fuel gauge for the hundredth time. The mountain was incredibly large.

"Miss Talmai," he said, "why the hell are we doing this, and what are you doing here in this plane?"

"It's not real, is it," she said, "and we're not even working for the same people."

Marsh grinned. "That's the trouble," he said. "You forget you're working—it's all part of the trap. Israel's relying on you and the British hope I turn up with the goods. We're getting paid but we've both forgotten we're working—we're doing this because we don't have any choice."

"We're getting higher," she said. "Stop talking and fly this thing. We've got to make it now."

He glanced quickly at her. "Buy you a dinner if we get there."

"Is that the best you can do?"

"No it's not, but you better say what you mean. I can't think of more than one thing at a time right now."

"I've already told you—I hate you," her voice was quite steady.

"That's fine. I hate you, too—but I wish you didn't look so good."

"Wait until we land."

Marsh nodded. "I intend to." He adjusted the radio

frequency wondering what the hell the American air-traffic organization were up to.

Seven and a half minutes later the situation had changed so dramatically that his curiosity at the silence of the Cessna's radio was instantly forgotten.

Sharmila saw the other aircraft first.

Two hundred feet above them, like a hawk shadowing its prey, it was overtaking them at no more than a few miles an hour difference in speed. Like the Cessna it was displaying no lights.

Sandwiched between the mountains below and the aircraft above, Marsh immediately banked the Cessna and began to climb into clear airspace where he would have more room to maneuver. The newcomer made no attempt to change course as if waiting for Marsh to draw alongside.

"Two guesses," Marsh said. "One of them's bound to be right." He knew the Canadian border had suddenly moved elusively further away.

"Use the radio," Sharmila urged. "There's no need to guess."

"Dahl wouldn't send a twin-engined light plane," Marsh said. "If he'd decided to be serious he'd have asked the USAF to escort us down somewhere. You're right, there's no need to guess. To be honest I'm not all that surprised. I was afraid this might happen."

"Use the radio, please Steven."

"Rule one," Marsh said. "Let the enemy make the first move. Don't be impatient, they're not here just to keep us company. There you are," he pointed at the larger plane through the perspex window in the door. A bright light was winking at them from the cockpit.

"You read it," Marsh said, "we're both flying too low. I need to watch the ground. They obviously don't want to use their radio either."

Sharmila waited until she had two complete words before speaking.

"Divert Chelan," she said. "My morse isn't too hot. Does that make sense?"

"Lake Chelan," Marsh explained. "Do they think we've got a bloody float plane."

"They're repeating the same words."

He reached forwards and flicked the wing-tip light switch for several seconds sending a request for the other aircraft to identify itself.

As if to answer, it immediately dropped back, the pilot putting it into a steep climb.

"Watch it, Sharmila," Marsh said, "don't let it out of your sight."

"It's still falling behind but it's much higher than us now." Her voice became more excited. "They're diving on us, Steven."

Marsh took a chance and glanced over his shoulder. Although a much larger and faster aircraft than the Cessna, even in a dive its speed of approach was not spectacular. He watched it come towards them.

The pilot was not going to attempt anything stupid, Marsh was sure of that. At such a dangerously low altitude both planes would wind up smashed to pieces on the rocky mountainsides below. The demonstration was for some other purpose.

Three hundred yards behind, the twin-engined plane flattened out and suddenly he understood. A series of bright orange flashes stabbed out towards him from the side of its nose.

Instinctively March wrenched at his controls to avoid the lethal stream of bullets. A fraction of a second later he realized he had reacted unnecessarily. The demonstration had been exactly that. A warning, a clear indication of superiority. He caught the Cessna and brought it back to level flight.

Sharmila was frightened. He had known her long enough to sense her tension even before she spoke. Marsh interrupted her before she could begin. "Our old friends don't give up easily, do they?"

In the dim glow inside the cockpit he could see her face. A face by now very familiar but still beautiful. A young girl who had thought they'd get to Canada, someone who should never have got involved in a lousy deal like this.

"So we're beaten," she said helplessly. "Call Air Traffic Control before it's too late. It'd be better for the CIA to have the drawings."

"No way," Marsh replied. "We'd be shot full of holes before anyone could get to us. If they can't persuade us to ditch on Lake Chelan they only have one other choice—push us down somewhere out of the way and have a go at getting hold of the drawings out of the wreckage. Always assuming we don't burn up of course. You can bet your life they've got people standing by at Chelan and they might even have a car or two hanging around our flight route just in case."

She reached out and placed her hand over his. "Then just get us back into the American radar network. Maybe Dahl will do something to stop us flying across the border."

Marsh shook his head. "You're underrating the opposition. Watch." He pulled back on the stick.

At once the other plane commenced another climb until it lay, talons sharp and ready, directly across the face of the moon. An armed escort of the night waiting for the opportunity to rip the frail Cessna into a thousand pieces before dumping it on the Cascades.

"They'll never get the drawings if they shoot us down now," Sharmila said. "Even a helicopter wouldn't find what would be left down there."

"So they know we won't try anything all the time we're flying over the mountains. Chelan is east of the Cascades—in the middle of the nearest thing Washington's got to desert country. Once we get away from here they'll be expecting us to play games but they're bargaining on forcing us all the way to the lake."

For the first time since he had met her, Marsh

thought he heard her swear. Unable to understand what she was saying, he supposed she was speaking Hebrew.

For a fleeting moment he experienced a wave of great tenderness and an overwhelming feeling of responsibility for what had happened. Unlike many men placed in his present position, Marsh did not yet accept the inevitability of losing what appeared to be a somewhat one-sided battle for the Israeli drawings and he was painfully aware that if he did, both he and the girl would pay with their lives. For a reason he had not encountered for many years, this time it was important to survive. The girl beside him had made the difference and he knew how dangerous that was. He endeavored to remind himself that she was a MOSSAD agent—decided that he was becoming soft and narrowly avoided a pinnacle of almost white rock which appeared frighteningly out of the moonlight.

"You should've jumped out when I told you to," he said. "You've left it a bit late now."

She bit her lip. "Be serious, please. You know what'll happen if we crash-land on the lake, don't you? After they've got the drawings, I mean."

"And I think you're underestimating me—my imagination's as good as yours." He wished he had an answer ready for her next question.

"What are we going to do?"

"I'll tell you in a minute. And you don't crash-land on water—the word is ditch. That's the trouble with you, your English is terrible."

Still forbidding, the Cascades seemed to consist of nothing other than one huge mountain after another interspersed with deep dark ravines and craggy rocks, all of them illuminated in harsh, cold moonlight. Not good country for anything, Marsh thought, but the first threads of an idea were beginning to form.

Maintaining the same distance from the escort aircraft, he studied it more closely, trying to recognize the type and seeing if he could estimate its size more accurately.

With the Cessna's fuel gauge showing a depressingly low level of precious gas and thoroughly outclassed by the other aircraft in both speed and armament, Marsh reluctantly abandoned the idea of even attempting to cross into Canada by air. Instead he would have to exploit the single slender advantage that the Cessna possessed, laying his trust in what he imagined must be a dwindling supply of Marsh luck. Insufficient time remained to originate more than one method of possible escape—he would have to be ready at any moment from now on. Mentally committed, he tried unsuccessfully to remember details of the Washington geography that lay ahead of them.

"Well?" Sharmila inquired, the strain very noticeable in her voice now.

"Do you trust me, Israeli girl?"

"Yes."

"Got any good ideas?" Marsh asked.

"No."

"Okay then. Just do what I say when I say it and hang on to that parcel of ours." He glanced again at the larger aircraft wondering about the machine-gun. Or a machine-pistol—perhaps nothing more than a fully automatic hand gun. There was no way for him to be certain. Not that it made a great deal of difference to his plan—just on their subsequent chances of getting out of this alive.

The moon was much higher now, shortening the shadows on the ground and making it marginally easier to determine the real height of the larger peaks. Flying over the eastern foothills, they were well away from the highest part of the Cascades already, allowing both planes to reduce their height above sea level as they made their way to the long, thin Washington lake called Chelan.

Three main highways had passed beneath the wheels

of the Cessna since it had left Mount Rainier but they were not heavily trafficked routes, only five or six sets of headlights appearing for the short time when the aircraft was overhead. From several thousand feet up Marsh knew the picture would be different, but at a mere hundred feet or so, the chances of spotting a vehicle were not good. In any event the highways he had seen were not suitable for what he had in mind. But he had not long to wait.

Eighteen miles from the lake and less than a hundred miles away from Canada, Marsh saw what he was looking for. He had only seconds in which to decide.

"Tighten your harness," he yelled, "we're going down."

He flicked the switch to turn on his wing-tip lights and shoved the Cessna into the tightest turn he thought it could stand. At the same time he opened the throttle wide feeling the prop bite at the air as the inevitable side slip began.

Let there be power poles, Marsh prayed. And let the surface be better than it had appeared from the first glimpse he'd had of the road.

The very fabric of the Cessna was shuddering from the severity of the maneuver but he had achieved what he had hoped to achieve.

Directly below the Cessna's fixed undercarriage, a narrow road was curving its way round a massive rock outcrop. And, in the finest American tradition, marching along one edge of the tarmacadam was an endless row of solid power poles.

There was no time to wait for the road to straighten and no time to find out what action the pilot of the other aircraft had taken.

Marsh wrenched the Cessna back from an overswing, trying frantically to match the curve in the road.

"Put your door on the half catch," he shouted.

In moonlight, with a rock escarpment on one side

and a power line on the other, Marsh made up his mind.

On full flap he pushed up the nose of the plane and hit the ignition switch. In a perfect stall the aircraft seemed to drop the last few feet. But the Cessna was traveling too fast and Marsh had attempted the impossible.

For several seconds after the undercarriage had smashed into the unforgiving road surface, he managed to hold it on the curve. Then as their speed decreased he felt the wandering begin. Desperately he fought for control.

The left hand wing grazed the rock face ripping aluminum alloy as though it were paper. Miraculously he prevented the plane from swerving further into the side but, as the wing-tip tore free, the Cessna shot across the narrow road as if launched from a catapult.

There was a single scream from the girl then the plane hit one of the wooden poles.

Impact took place almost immediately at the wing root, one of the strongest areas of the aircraft and the location of a main gas tank.

Part of the fuselage disintegrated leaving the smashed wing attached to it by nothing more than trailing steel control cables. From one side of the road to the other aviation fuel sprayed from the ruptured tank igniting in a huge streak of orange flame.

Surrounded by minor wreckage where the Cessna had crashed into it, strangely, the pole remained upright in the ground. What remained of the shattered aircraft careered wildly onwards until its surviving wing plowed deeply into the ground spilling the fuselage to a final halt in a series of giant lurches.

A line of fire twenty feet high reached from the power pole to the gaping wound in the side of the plane but mercifully there had been insufficient fuel to cause a major conflagration and, by the time the

Cessna had come to rest, the worst of the blaze was over.

Severely shocked and terribly bruised, a man and woman staggered from the wreckage to stand fifty yards from the road where the plane had tried to land. After the awful noise of a moment ago it was very quiet.

"Jesus," Marsh said weakly, "are you all right?"

Her answer was cut short by the roar of a diving aircraft. It was heading directly for them.

Half staggering and half running, Marsh pulled her back to the roadside where, with the whine of the propellers echoing in their ears, the harsh stammer of the machine-gun filled the night with a new sound.

To their right, puffs of soil erupted in a long line along the verge.

"Get over by the rock face," Marsh yelled at her. "See if you can find somewhere safe." He followed the plane against the moon watching it climb, turn and approach for the second time.

Hoping the pilot would make a mistake and fly straight into the ground in his enthusiasm to finish off the destruction which Marsh had begun, he sprinted across the road to join Sharmila.

Again the chatter of the gun told them of the extreme danger they were in, yet again they escaped unscathed.

"You're mad," she sobbed. "You nearly killed us."

Above the roar of the retreating plane Marsh yelled back at her. "But I didn't and the bastards can't land because of their wingspan. All we have to do is find some cover and wait until they give up."

But as the aircraft turned once more, he realized despairingly that there was nowhere for them to hide. Outlined against the rock in full moonlight Marsh saw the dive begin.

CHAPTER NINE

Four men walked briskly from the car to the unprepossessing front door of the Israeli embassy. Three of them formed a protective triangle for the fourth, a large man wearing a dark expression of unconcealed annoyance.

It was preposterous, John Reylord fumed, bloody preposterous. Two o'clock on a sunny September afternoon in the heart of London yet they thought it necessary to provide a guard. What the hell did they expect to happen.

At the door, one of the men pushed the button for him. It was all Reylord could do to prevent himself from shoving his escort rudely out of the way.

A neatly dressed middle-aged woman answered the bell and announced that Mr. Reylord was expected. He entered the embassy at once, pointedly ignoring the presence of the three other men who remained outside.

He apologized for being a few minutes early for the appointment. "I hope you don't mind," he said easily. "I would be very grateful for a cup of coffee whilst I wait—I'm afraid my lunch was rather rushed."

The woman politely returned his smile. "I'm sure Colonel Yaacobi would take it as a compliment if you were to join him at once," she said. "I will be pleased to bring your coffee to the conference room. If you would be so kind as to follow me."

Reylord trailed her up a short flight of carpeted

stairs and along a musty smelling corridor to a wood paneled door at the end.

The Colonel rose to meet him. "It's been a long time, John," he said in perfect English. "I last shook hands with you in New York nearly two years ago."

With seating capacity for twenty people, the embassy conference room was not the ideal venue for such a meeting, Reylord thought. He waited until the door closed behind him before speaking. Despite the cordiality of Yaacobi's greeting he knew the Colonel was displeased to see him. In his position he would undoubtedly have been experiencing the same regrets.

Reylord tossed a slim briefcase on to the table. "I imagine we can speak freely?" he inquired.

"I hardly believe Israel has much more to lose on this particular matter," Yaacobi replied. "You would like something to drink?"

"I've already asked for a coffee, thank you—are you sure you're not being too pessimistic, Itzhak? As I understand it things could have turned out to be a good deal worse for you."

Yaacobi sat down at one end of the table indicating for Reylord to make himself comfortable. "I've already been given a suitably edited account of how the CIA have fallen over backwards in their efforts to obtain our drawings." The irony in his voice could not be missed.

"You know I'm representing the United States Government in this, don't you?" Reylord said. "The drawings were flown over by the U.S. Air Force and delivered directly to the American embassy here in London." Reylord cleared his throat and assumed a deliberately tactful expression. "The British have not been involved apart from expressing their gratitude of course."

The Colonel smiled softly. "Thank you for that but I regret my pessimism remains. Tell me, how is it that you wear two hats nowadays, my friend?"

Reylord stared out of the window for a moment. "I

am employed as energy adviser to NATO and as such I am usually committed to NATO projects. At present, as you know, I am based in London responsible for leading an inquiry into the Federation of Anglo-American Companies in an endeavor to discover the identities of twelve organizations who have caused the west a great deal of embarrassment."

"And who have caused Israel to lose one of her most important military secrets," Yaacobi said bitterly. "But today you represent the United States only?"

"The Kfir drawings were flown to London so I would have the opportunity of talking to you. I cannot leave England for at least another week. Yes Colonel, today, or rather this afternoon, I am an emissary not of NATO but of the United States Government."

Yaacobi nodded. "So Israel must express her appreciation for the recovery of our drawings. The British discover who have stolen them, the Americans find them for us and the CIA have of course naturally avoided the temptation to examine them."

The window was attracting Reylord's attention again. "I can't answer that."

"If the Arabs or the Soviets are given copies Israel will know very well how they received the information."

"The United States have safeguarded Israel's interests by avoiding the involvement of the British," Reylord reminded him. "I consider your statement to be unnecessarily provocative."

Colonel Yaacobi looked him squarely in the eyes. "Oil, my friend, is a very provocative subject, but I have spoken unwisely. Israel is grateful for American assistance as always—you will forget what I have said?"

Reylord thought that they were both playing with words. But there was no other way. He wished he knew what the White House would decide to do with the photocopies of the drawings they had undoubtedly taken. Yaacobi was fully aware that the CIA must have examined the drawings but Reylord could do nothing either to confirm or deny it without appearing to be a fool. And John Reylord was not a fool.

Coffee disturbed further fencing on the subject. Reylord lit a cigarette whilst the Colonel opened the briefcase and spilled out the contents on to the table top. As he did so he wondered how hard the girl had tried and reflected on the futility of sending one MOSSAD agent to combat the entire CIA. He had heard nothing from her for over a week now—a waste of time and money, maybe a waste of another Israeli life. It was difficult to keep his bitterness from rising to the surface.

Unfolding the drawings he stared blankly at them, finding it hard to believe that such ordinary pieces of paper could so easily affect the future of his country. Following the instructions he had received before leaving Jerusalem he ran his fingers casually over the top right hand corner of one sheet searching for the three pin pricks. There were none.

He folded the drawing with care then drew another one in front of him pretending to study it. His brain was racing.

"Everything all right?" Reylord inquired interestedly.

"Same as the copies I was shown but I'm no electronics expert, John." The Colonel strove to keep his voice level.

He picked up the new sheet by its top corners as if to inspect it more closely. No pin pricks brushed his exploring finger tip. Moving his hands casually down the edge of the paper, he gripped the lower edge prior to refolding it. There was no doubt. The drawing was devoid of identifying punctures.

Colonel Yaacobi tried to think. One pinprick for restricted, two for secret and three for top secret. But these drawings had none.

Sliding the drawings into a heap he placed them to

one side on the table. His hands trembled imperceptibly.

"It is a great pity we did not intercept these before they left Israel," he said, "but I am relieved that they did not reach the Arabs."

Reylord nodded. "So am I. I have been asked to formally tell you that the United States are pleased to have been able to help Israel in this way."

Yaacobi smiled, his eyes revealing nothing of what was passing through his mind. "And in return," he said, "I must formally express the gratitude of the Jewish nation for a further demonstration of the friendship which exists between our two countries."

Reylord's tone changed. "Okay," he said. "Now all that crap's over with can we get down to business?"

"You have nothing more to discuss concerning the hand-over of these drawings?"

"No," Reylord said. "I want to put my NATO hat back on and ask you some questions about your missile design establishment."

The Colonel sighed. "You still believe you will not be able to trace these Western Companies without linking them to someone working inside Israel?"

"We've made some progress in our investigation," Reylord answered, "and now we've got enough teeth to break any organization which refuses to co-operate. The Federation of Anglo-American Companies has even offered to provide their own inquiry team. Their president started off by being a clever bastard but a little pressure soon changed that."

"Your Mr. Dryden," Yaacobi commented sourly, "he is no friend of the Jews."

"He doesn't pretend to be but he's not stupid enough to organize something like this. Dryden is influenced by money and position not anti-semitism."

"You are presupposing Dryden has not been bought?" The Colonel's voice was heavy with cynicism.

"We're not presupposing anything, Itzhak, but Dryden appears to be clean and we've been very thorough. Nevertheless he is still under surveillance."

Colonel Yaacobi was extremely anxious to bring this meeting to a close. What had gone wrong? Or had perhaps something gone right? There was much work for him to do, telephone calls to make and a great deal of analysis to undertake on these drawings Reylord had delivered.

He stood up and walked to the far end of the long glass-topped table, unable to prevent himself from recalling the pretty eager face of Sharmila Talmai when she had been briefed. Where was she? Had the girl lived up to his expectations after all or were the Americans trying another one of their ingenious international tricks? There was no way to begin even considering methods of obtaining answers until Reylord had departed.

"I await your questions John," Yaacobi said. "But we have previously attempted to find out if some of the blame can be attributed to an element which exists inside my own country. Your people already know everything which might be of assistance."

And if I don't get a lead pretty soon, Reylord thought, while CIA copies are secretly leaked to the Arabs under the guise of maintaining the balance of power in the Middle East, Lance Dryden's renegade companies will be trying again. The feeling of being used was stronger than it had been for some days—aggravated by the fact that Yaacobi had virtually suggested American ethics were no longer to be trusted. Almost overnight the international struggle for oil had further condemned Israel and turned the United States into a nation of split responsibilities.

John Reylord began talking, endeavoring to learn something new which would expose the names of the companies which the west were searching for. After an hour of fruitless conversation he made ready to bid the Colonel farewell.

"I am of course not officially in London," Yaacobi said dryly. "You understand?"

Reylord stuck out a large hand. "As soon as I have something definite you'll hear through the normal channels," he said. "Perhaps when we next meet things will be better for Israel."

"They will have to be," Yaacobi replied. "And if we do not see each other for another two years I can assure you the Middle East situation will be much changed in our favor. We are a very tenacious race, John. I will see you to the door. Thank you for coming yourself—I understand your difficulties better than you imagine."

Two minutes later Reylord was on his way back to the American embassy. The men who had accompanied him on his journey to deliver the drawings were nowhere to be seen.

Back in the embassy conference room Colonel Yaacobi was soon painstakingly examining the upper right hand corner of each drawing with the aid of a powerful magnifying glass. It took him only seconds to determine that they were neither copies nor the originals he had expected to receive.

Having no way of identifying the technical content of the complex drawings before him—for he had not bothered to take the precaution of familiarizing himself with the Kfir design details before flying to London —he was now certain that his immediate return to Jerusalem was of vital importance. But first he must try to contact the girl.

Collecting the pile of drawings, he left the empty room and returned to his temporary office where he began composing a memo to a colleague in the New York embassy.

Although the girl had last been heard of on the West Coast, Yaacobi had already decided on the wisdom of asking America's largest Jewish embassy to assist him in his search. If they were unable to provide a lead it would be necessary to send someone else over to carry out an urgent investigation. Either that or embark upon a frustrating wait until he did receive some news. Yaacobi was not a patient man.

He pressed a button on his telephone, summoning one of the senior embassy aides.

A young man entered the office almost at once. The Colonel passed him the memo. "By coded telex to New York," he said. "Please bring me the answer as soon as you have translated it."

Yaacobi had picked up his phone before the aide had closed the door. He asked for an open line to Tel Aviv.

Whilst he waited he listed the numbers of the drawings on his blotter and spread open one sheet on his desk.

"Five," the Colonel said shortly into the receiver, "thirty-two David."

Seconds later, speaking to one of his MOSSAD contacts, he read out the list of numbers and then provided a remarkably accurate description of the single drawing in front of him.

"I want an open telex reply inside the next hour," Yaacobi said, "and tell my wife I'm leaving London tomorrow."

For the next fifteen minutes, Colonel Yaacobi endeavored to sift through the large number of confusing scraps of information which he had acquired so far. The task was by no means easy.

Of one thing he was certain. Neither the CIA nor the American Government had any idea that the drawings were not genuine. But if these pieces of paper were not drawings of the Kfir missile what were they? For some obscure and possibly dangerous reason someone seemed very anxious to deceive the Americans.

He was still wrestling with the problem when his reply from Tel Aviv was brought to the office. The telex was not only brief but startlingly clear in content.

DRAWINGS UNIDENTIFIABLE. ISRAELI ORIGIN DOUBT-
FUL.

The Colonel examined the sheets for the third time. No engineer, he was neither able to decipher the function of the parts nor read the complicated circuit diagrams. A feeling of inadequacy began to creep over him and he was conscious of being particularly alone in his mission of unraveling the mystery which John Reylord had so unwittingly presented to him.

When the aide delivered the long answer from New York the matter appeared to be less confused but Yaacobi knew the picture was still hopelessly incomplete. He read the telex again.

MAX NAVON FOUND DEAD NEVADA DESERT YESTERDAY. OFFICIAL CAUSE OF DEATH SNAKE BITE. NO FURTHER DATA AVAILABLE.

TELEPHONE COMMUNICATION RECEIVED FROM TALMAI WHILST UNDER CUSTODY OF CIA IN SAN FRANCISCO BUT MESSAGE UNCLEAR. CIA HAVE ASKED FOR FULL DETAILS OF REASON FOR TALMAI U.S. VISIT. UNCONFIRMED REPORT OF TALMAI IN COMPANY OF STEVEN MARSH SUSPECTED BRITISH AGENT. CIA REFUSE TO REVEAL PRESENT WHEREABOUTS OF GIRL.

MARSH MAY HAVE FLOWN LIGHT AIRCRAFT FROM RENO TO UNKNOWN DESTINATION WITHIN LAST 24 HRS. ACCORDING TO REPORT RECEIVED FROM CONTACT MONITORING ATC RADIO FREQUENCY. RELIABILITY OF THIS DATA YET TO BE DETERMINED.

TALMAI—NAVON LINK UNQUESTIONABLE. WILL CONCENTRATE FURTHER INQUIRIES IN NEVADA IMMEDIATELY.

SUGGEST TALMAI MAY BE SLEEPER. REQUEST LONDON INVESTIGATE STEVEN MARSH ON YOUR BEHALF.

TRUST U.S. HAVE HANDED OVER KFIR MISSILE DATA AS PROMISED. DOUBT CIA INTEGRITY BUT YOU ARE AWARE OF OFFICIAL VIEW ON THIS.

The Colonel grunted to himself at the last sentence, wondering why New York found it necessary to remind him of something which was one of the main reasons for his own involvement in an otherwise relatively straightforward job.

So the girl had not completely disappeared—had not vanished as other MOSSAD agents had. But whether or not she could offer an explanation for the set of drawings on his desk remained to be seen. It was an academic question at present and the Colonel wasted no time on speculation. Instead, whilst he was here in London, the embassy could see if they could discover the whereabouts of Mr. Steven Marsh for him.

He called for the aide again.

CHAPTER TEN

Shortly after Marsh saw the plane turn at the top of its climb prior to beginning its third run, he was gripped with an anger so great that all fear was immediately dispelled. His abduction from the motel, his trial with the rattlesnake, a narrow escape during takeoff and now this. Having miraculously survived the landing, Marsh was not going to be cheated now.

The dying line of flames was acting as a perfect pointer to their position and standing helplessly with their backs to the rock in bright moonlight could do nothing but assist the gunner in his deadly mission.

Swiftly Marsh assessed the speed of the plane. Eight seconds, maybe nine.

"Come on," he yelled to Sharmila. "Hit the dirt when I shout."

Seizing her hand he pulled her after him along the dusty verge, the scream of the attacking aircraft increasing with each stumbling step.

Only someone of Marsh's caliber could have done it. With every nerve in his body telling him to flatten himself on the ground he kept running, expecting the deathly chatter to begin before he had executed his bluff.

By now the pilot would have them lined up in his sights watching them like a couple of scuttling ants. Five, six, Marsh counted. Now!

"Back across the road," he yelled, swinging the girl

wildly on to the harder surface by her arm. Horribly exposed they raced to the other side.

"Down, down," he shouted, flinging both of them headlong into the sand and gravel.

Mouth and nose filled with choking grit he heard the machine-gun spit out another lethal stream of lead.

Marsh rolled over to watch bullets ricocheting off the rock face and tearing long furrows in the scrubby grass across the road. Had they kept running along the base of the escarpment, that's where they'd have stayed—a bloody mess where two people had been shredded to pieces.

Sharmila had quite obviously had enough. The awful shock of the Cessna's crash-landing had numbed her and there had been no opportunity for her to recover. Now, after being relentlessly pursued by the aircraft, her eyes were wide with terror. Like Marsh, she too had thrown herself down in a frantic attempt to evade the bullets, making no effort to cushion her fall. Her breasts painfully bruised and blood pouring from a split lip she gazed at him as if for help. In her left hand she held a tattered parcel.

Marsh felt his anger surge. One day—not far from now—someone was going to pay for this. He had been pushed around long enough.

He could still hear the aircraft but for a second he was not able to see it against the sky. They would try again—and again but each time there would be a brief period of respite during which Marsh could search for cover.

Tenderly he lifted her to her feet. "We've got to move," he said. "They can still see us and they'll be coming back." He wiped the blood from her mouth and took the parcel from her. "Come on, this rock won't go on forever—just a little further and we'll be safe."

Tugging her along by the hand again, he set off down the road, relying on his ears to tell him when the next attack would be. With his eyes he searched for some crack or crevice in which they could shelter.

They had traveled less than fifty yards when Marsh heard a new noise. Almost before he had decided on the source, headlights swept round the curve ahead of them. At once he dragged Sharmila into the center of the road and began waving his arms.

A truck—a huge, interstate diesel. Marsh could hardly believe their luck. There was the hiss of pneumatic brakes and the grinding of gears. It stopped only a few feet from where they stood.

He ran forward to the cab. "Car accident," he said through the two inch gap in the window that the driver offered. "My wife's hurt but not too badly. Can you give us a ride, please?"

Hurry, Marsh breathed. For Christ's sake hurry or we're all dead.

A flashlight shone in his face then flicked down to Sharmila leaning weakly against the front mudguard. She looked up blinking.

"Okay, mister. Get round the other side." The driver had decided.

With the big diesel rumbling only inches away Marsh had no idea where the plane might be. Would they dare try to stop the truck?

He lifted Sharmila on to the first step, placing her hands on the rungs of the short ladder. "Quickly," he whispered, "or we'll be late for that dinner I promised you."

Climbing in after her, he spared a rapid glance into the blackness surrounding the glow from the truck's lights, but could see nothing. He slammed the door shut.

"Thanks very much," Marsh said. "I know you're not supposed to stop and I suppose we don't look all that respectable either."

"If you wanta hijack this rig you're welcome, I'm hauling aircraft parts—not much of a blackmarket for

them." The driver started winding his way up steadily
through his gears. " 'Course the truck's worth a bit but
it belongs to Boeing in Seattle not me."

Any minute now, Marsh thought, deciding to take
the bull by the horns. But before he could speak, their
headlights rounded a bend to illuminate the littered
wreckage of the Cessna. Some distance away from the
wingless fuselage two small fires remained burning, the
smoke curling vertically upwards towards the moon.

As the driver applied his brakes Marsh leaned across
the seat. "It's okay," he said, "that was us. I said it
was a car accident to save time."

Still the truck slowed. "Don't stop," Sharmila said
urgently. "Please don't stop—there was no one else in
it. Just keep going."

The driver seemed unconvinced. "What's the goddam hurry?" he inquired suspiciously.

"The hurry," Marsh said, "is because if you don't
get this bloody truck moving we will very likely all
wind up dead." He watched the driver's expression
harden. "It's not a hijack. That is, or was, our plane
and I'll explain everything in a minute, but keep rolling
while I talk—I'm serious about the danger. Come on—
move."

"Mister, if this is a joke you've sure got hold of the
wrong guy." He inspected his watch. "If I don't radio
in eighteen minutes' time they'll send a tracer out for
this truck. That don't leave you much time for whatever you have in mind."

Marsh breathed more easily as the truck picked up
speed again. Somewhere high above them in the dark
an armed aircraft was playing a waiting game, the men
that manned it probably trying to decide on their next
move.

A sudden chill spread over Marsh. "What did you
say you were carrying?" he said.

"What the hell does it matter—you better start talking;" the driver sounded as though his patience was exhausted.

"Airframe parts," Marsh said. "Airframe parts."

"What of it?"

"Magnesium alloy?" Marsh inquired quietly.

"Yeah, some of them."

"Oh Jesus," Marsh breathed. "Now you listen. We were forced down on the road by another aircraft carrying a machine-gun. You might find that hard to believe but unless you do, we're in trouble. The same aircraft knows we're in this truck and you can bet your sweet life it's up there following us right now. If they decide they might just as well wreck your truck now they've started getting really tough, they'll be along any time to shoot us full of holes. Do you have the picture?"

The driver remained silent as if contemplating the prospect of having his truck shot full of holes.

"Magnesium," Marsh repeated, in case the point had been missed. "The men in that aircraft don't know you're carrying aircraft parts."

"Takes a lot to get it going"—the driver spoke gruffly.

"Yes, it does," Marsh agreed. "But how about driving without lights so we don't risk finding out how much it does take. I'd hate to be part of a flash bulb this big."

"They'll aim for the cab," Sharmila said. "We'd miss seeing the flash by just a little while." She spoke through the handkerchief she was holding to her mouth. "It will be more difficult for them if we are without headlights."

Traveling in more open country now, the driver switched off his lights without the need for further persuasion. At the same time he increased his speed until twenty tons of tractor and trailer were thundering along through the moonlight at nearly seventy miles an hour.

"I'll radio," he announced. "You'd better tell me what this is all about."

Out of nowhere, like a huge black bat, the aircraft roared over the truck only feet above the top of the cab. Added to the beating from the diesel the noise was tremendous.

Sharmila buried her head on Marsh's arm.

"That's them," Marsh said grimly. "Your radio isn't going to help."

"Spotlight," the driver said shortly. "Special one. Three hundred and twenty-five watt beam." He pointed to a lever protruding from the roof. "Blow your eyes out in the dark. I've used it a couple of times on high-way cowboys—sends them straight off the road."

Marsh became immediately interested. "They'll come at us directly from the front," he said. "My wife was right, they'll aim at the cab. It might work if we see them coming early enough."

"The moon is ahead of us," Sharmila said, sitting up straight, "they will fly using the road to find us."

Marsh grunted. An aircraft diving at perhaps two hundred miles an hour combined with a moving truck at seventy produced an awesome closing speed of two hundred and seventy. But the aircraft gunner would be faced with exactly the same problem.

Steadying himself with the grab handle, Marsh stood up to investigate the spot lamp control more closely. A small hand clamped down on his wrist. "I'll do it," Sharmila said. "This one is for me."

"Sit down," Marsh told her, "you're in no shape for anything."

Big eyes stared into his. "Twelve weeks' night train-ing," she said firmly, "rated as having exceptional night vision and best in group at instinctive weapon aiming. Do you still want to argue?"

Marsh sat down. "I should've let you land the plane," he said.

She shook her head. "I can't fly."

"I'm not sure I can anymore either," Marsh replied.

"You know what to do, don't you?" His own eyes were in very poor shape and perhaps she was right.

She leaned forward slightly, gripping the T-bar handle, her eyes fixed ahead. She said nothing.

The driver switched off the lights on his instrument panel and edged the truck over to the center of the road. "Should've left you where I found you," he said. "How do I know you're not talking a lot of crap. Why should anyone want to make you crash?"

"Long story," Marsh said shortly. "Just drive until this is over with. If you see them first—yell." More than anything in the world he wanted to push Sharmila out of the way and seize the spot lamp lever himself. Three hundred and twenty-five watts against an airborne machine-gun—a poor match by any standard but it was all they had.

Stopping the truck now would allow them to temporarily escape by foot if they chose the spot carefully but Marsh knew there was bound to be a car on its way from Chelan or closer and he preferred to take his chances on the move. He strained tired eyes into the night searching for the vague outline of a low flying plane.

Rounding a fast right hand curve the truck entered a long empty straight flanked on one side by a tall pine forest. Background illumination provided by the moon was barely adequate at the speed they were now traveling.

As she had before earlier on this same night, Sharmila saw the attacker first. She uttered a single word then focused her entire attention on the dark phantom she had glimpsed high above the tree tops.

Two miles away, the pilot made his descent towards the large square target coming directly towards him. He too was tired and his eyes sore from several hours spent in the kind of flying that ordinarily no sane man would attempt. Anxious to finish things so his colleagues could collect the drawings once their car arrived here, he expertly aligned the nose of his aircraft with the road two hundred feet below. In the other front seat another man lined up the sights of his automatic weapon.

A Viet Nam veteran, the truck driver wondered whether two grown men should be trusting their lives to the slim young girl kneeling between them on the seat. He also wondered if he was being particularly stupid.

At five miles a minute, truck and aircraft screamed towards each other along the highway.

Memories of a desert range far away in Israel formed a thin backdrop to the girl's fierce concentration.

Now, Marsh breathed. Sharmila squeezed the switch.

Fifteen feet too high, a concentrated beam of pure white light was driven outwards into the darkness. With perfect control Sharmila brought it a few minutes of arc lower, centering it precisely on the windshield of the approaching plane.

Caught unawares, totally blinded, the pilot reacted in the only possible way, putting his aircraft into a punishing climb to evade the brilliant light.

Like a desperate Englishman some hours earlier on this tragic night, he too had misjudged the ability of his plane. And like the unfortunate Cessna, his wingtip had insufficient clearance. Not solid rock but the slender branch of pine brushed across it.

Under ordinary circumstances such gentle contact would have been of little significance but circumstances were far from normal for intense white light was still flooding the cockpit making it impossible for the pilot to establish any frame of reference. Spatially disoriented he increased his angle of climb.

Behind him another man was screaming something and beside him, similarly dazzled, in a useless gesture the man with the machine-gun raised his hands in front of him as if to push away the beam.

The trivial collision with the branch was a prelude to complete disaster. The pilot had no second chance.

Still traveling at two hundred miles an hour, the aircraft appeared to flip on to its back before being swallowed up by the forest.

Long after the truck had passed the point where it had disappeared, a column of fire spiraled skywards out of the trees to mark where plane and occupants had died.

"Keep moving," Marsh instructed, helping Sharmila gently back on to the seat. "There's nothing we can do." He could feel her trembling.

Reducing speed, the driver shivered once as if awakening from a dream. "Some guys pick up queers, some take a fancy to a girl and find themselves on a rape charge. Me—I have to pick up you. You'd better have a real good story for all this, mister—and the little lady here. She shot that aircraft down like she was using a .30-millimeter cannon. Who the hell are you?" He switched on all of his lights and squinted across the cab at his passengers.

For a second Marsh had been with the pilot of the aircraft. There but for the grace of God, he thought, knowing that his own narrow escape in crash-landing the Cessna was something he would never forget. He experienced no regret, no remorse at killing the men who had attacked them. They had died trying to murder the three people in this truck and retribution had been swift, unforgiving and entirely just. Yet it had been the Israeli girl—Sharmila—who had killed them. Killed them as surely as if she had been behind the sights of a gun just as the truck driver had said. And she had wanted to do it.

Marsh put an arm round her. "I'm sorry as hell about this," he said to the driver. "We're working for the CIA and I can't tell you much. It'd be better for you if you dropped us off and forgot what you've seen tonight. I don't recommend involvement with the CIA, they don't let go once they've started—not ever."

"Nice easy way out," the driver replied caustically. "Let me see your identification or did you leave it at home."

"Just drop us somewhere," Sharmila said quietly. "I am afraid you have no choice if you want to avoid trouble."

"Just forget all about it?" the driver was unwilling to consider the suggestion. "You really expect me to forget about it?"

"Okay," Marsh said, "use your radio. Explain what's happened. You'll have a dozen State Police on the road inside half a minute. Air Traffic Control will turn you inside out and if we don't back up your story you're likely to stay that way. If we want to we can say we saw you flash an SOS while we were flying over the Cascades. When we got low you blinded us with the light and we crashed. When they find that other aircraft they're going to start wondering about you. Maybe you've got a thing about bright lights or perhaps someone took away your toys when you were young. Not many trucks have searchlights fitted like yours. You're a pretty strange guy all round."

"You're going to be sensible, aren't you?" Sharmila asked him.

There was a moment's pause before the driver answered. Marsh hoped he wasn't going to become awkward.

"You'll keep quiet?" the driver said eventually, his voice full of doubt.

"We've got nothing to say," Sharmila told him. "And thank you. If you hadn't stopped for us we would be dead. We'll just disappear and you'll just forget. There is no other way, is there?"

The headlights of a rapidly moving vehicle appeared half a mile ahead. Marsh watched them draw closer, his doubt magnifying as they increased in size. Without slackening speed a car tore past them, vanishing seconds later into the blackness behind the truck.

"Where do you want to go?" the driver asked.

"Just take us wherever you're going," Marsh replied. "As long as it's a decent-sized town."

"Mister, I'm supposed to be in Seattle inside the next hour and a half. You want to go all the way?"

If some smart bastard doesn't try and stop us before we get there, Marsh thought, still sure the aircraft would have radioed information on its position to men at Lake Chelan before it crashed.

"Seattle will be fine," Marsh said. "You'd better check in on your radio otherwise they'll be sending out that tracer you mentioned."

"You don't wanta believe everything people tell you," the driver remarked, his voice more level. "That's my trouble, I'm a believer and look where it's got me."

"Change jobs with you," Marsh said, relieved at the change in tone.

"Your girl friend part of the deal?"

Marsh grinned—"Ask her."

There was sufficient light in the cab for him to see her face. Sharmila tried to smile, discovered it hurt her lip and decided against it.

"You've got it wrong," she said. "Like the man said, I'm his wife and anyway my husband is a terrible driver—you saw what he did to our plane."

So she's okay again, Marsh thought. Or at least the worst of the shock has passed. Her voice was far from normal but she was playing her part as he had seen her do before. Although there had already been plenty of opportunity for him to decide, he still wondered how tough she really was.

With the Joplin rendering of "Me and Bobby McGee" running stupidly through his head Marsh waited for the truck driver to take them all the way to Seattle.

CHAPTER ELEVEN

Almost unnoticed their relationship had changed in a subtle way. All wariness had finally gone and something much deeper had taken the place of the comradeship which had been binding them inexorably closer and closer together since they had first met.

Comradeship, Marsh thought wryly, was not really the word for what had existed before. Unaccustomed to sharing danger with a woman he was not altogether sure how the change had taken place but there was no doubt at all that he felt very differently about her.

He treated himself to another half a glass of bourbon and lit a cigarette from the glowing end of the one already held in his fingers. A man of well-developed sensitivity, he was confident that he had not mistaken the nature of Sharmila's recent attitude towards him. He had been unusually conscious of her presence as a woman ever since they had booked into the hotel, and although Marsh knew he should be fighting the idea of even the slightest involvement with her, he felt strangely elated at the prospect of their further association, almost eager to learn where the future was leading them.

The hotel room was by no means as opulent as some which Seattle had to offer, but, for two exhausted travelers requiring no more than somewhere to catch up on several nights of missed sleep, it approached the utmost in luxury.

Situated not far from the still busy main down-town center, they had booked in here an hour ago having used a taxi to transport them from Renton at the southern end of the city where the truck driver had left them. Tired and dirty, they had hardly spoken since their arrival, Sharmila falling asleep on the bed almost at once. She had woken ten minutes ago to stagger to the bathroom leaving Marsh slumped in his chair with only his thoughts for company.

No cars had attempted to waylay the truck on the final leg of its journey and Marsh was fairly certain they had managed to elude their pursuers temporarily or even permanently. It would take Dahl a very long time to discover what had happened out there on the highway and, with the remains of two wrecked aircraft to confuse matters, even the CIA would have their hands full in the inevitable investigation which would follow their discovery.

Providing the truck had not been shadowed as Marsh had initially feared, whoever had been waiting for the Cessna to ditch on Lake Chelan had lost the scent. For some reason or another the men who had come so very close to retrieving the Israeli drawings had completely missed their chance. For a while Steven Marsh and Sharmila Talmai were safe and the feeling was wonderful.

He let the bourbon roll around his mouth switching his thoughts back to the pretty girl still in the shower. Without the opportunity to consider the deal she had offered him in any depth since leaving San Francisco it was hard to switch off to let his mind relax and, for the moment, it was proving impossible to think of anything except the curious way their attitudes were changing towards each other.

Not just an attractive girl with a firm young body to make any man consider his chances. Not just a standard well-trained MOSSAD expert who had become hopelessly entangled in Marsh's own assignment, but a self-assured and desirable woman who treated him coolly as an equal one minute then, before he could catch his breath, turned into someone anxious or even desperate for his help and understanding.

His earlier ideas of giving her the slip already seemed unthinkable and, if such a thing was possible when their interests lay in somewhat different directions, he knew now that they would have to finish the project together. Or would they? And if Marsh had misjudged her—then what?

Sliding further back in his chair he closed his eyes and made the wish he reserved for occasions such as this. To hell with British Intelligence, to hell with the Middle East problem and to hell with his job. The wish was an old friend, a familiar desire to be his own man instead of an obedient puppet controlled with invisible strings by unseen men in London.

Once, Steven Marsh had enjoyed the unlimited expense accounts, the excitement and danger which were part of each assignment. Perhaps fifty women had drifted easily into his life during the last eight years, women Marsh had enjoyed almost as a matter of routine before they vanished just as easily into the past. But this assignment had turned into rather more than an assignment. Sharmila could not be deserted, he was thus unable to carry out instructions and Marsh was irritated at his own muddled feelings about the Israeli girl. Not just another woman—unless he could persuade himself to treat her as one.

Unable to divorce the responsibilities of his job from the bond which had grown, much against his wishes, between him and the girl who had so unexpectedly entered his life, he reached out for his drink again.

The gentle hiss of water from the shower stopped and he heard the click of the bathroom door.

Wrapped in a pale blue towel she stood before him her pretty mouth distorted by the cut on her lower lip.

"Go away," Marsh said. "For Christ's sake go away."

"Because you hate me, because I'm a real person or because you've had too much to drink?"

"Just go away"—Marsh sounded as if he meant it.

She sat down on the arm of his chair and helped herself to a drink from his glass. He could smell her freshness.

"You're tired, Steven," she said, staring into the distance.

He took the bottle of bourbon and drank from it. "Two days ago I had this whole damned thing sewn up," he said quietly. "I was happy, Dahl was happy and, if they'd known about it, London would've been happy. Then you came along. Yes I'm tired, very tired."

"And you are no longer happy?"

And you are no longer staring at the wall on the other side of the room Marsh observed, wondering what on earth it was about her that made it impossible for him to regard this as nothing more than another casual encounter with another woman. He considered her question.

"Sit somewhere else," he said. "I'm not that tired —and give me back my glass. If it makes any difference to anything I am not unhappy—I am glad we made it this far."

"So am I." She topped up his drink and passed it to him. "But dinner in Canada would have been nice. I was looking forward to that."

"Tomorrow," Marsh said. "Be glad we're not smeared all over the ground somewhere. I'll buy you dinner when we get there like I promised."

"I'm hungry now, Steven."

He groaned. "Okay, I'll call room service."

"What is the matter?" Her eyes were enormous.

Marsh levered himself up out of his chair to stand in front of her.

"You know bloody well what the matter is," he said evenly. "I've been sitting down thinking whilst you've been in the shower and all that happens is that I go round in circles. I'm not used to that."

She stood up to face him holding the towel. "Then give me the drawings and I'll go tonight." Her voice was suddenly tight.

Doubt surged through him. God, could he have been wrong after all?

"They're on the bed," he said. "Send Israel's part of the deal to London with my compliments." As he spoke he knew he was going to stop her. But still he could not bring himself to believe he had been such a fool and something was telling him it was important to declare himself now before the situation got out of hand.

"Hope you make it," he said carefully. "But before you go, I want you to know I'll never forget you, Sharmila."

He turned away from her.

She grabbed his shirt pulling him back.

"Is that it?" she said fiercely.

"What?"

"What I've been waiting to hear." Her eyes were softening and now he could not look away.

Marsh changed his mind again, reaching out to place his hands on her bare shoulders. "Do you remember what I said about forgetting you're working sometimes?" he said. "Perhaps I could make it clearer by saying that tonight, a little while ago, I wanted to forget. I even figured something might make forgetting pretty easy. But I'm still not sure if I've understood things properly."

For a second she remained quite still. Then she removed his hands one at a time as if deliberately breaking the contact he had established. Marsh waited.

Tears filled her eyes. "I too was not sure, but—"

He caught her in his arms as she fell towards him. This time, where his hands touched her skin, it was as if she was on fire.

For a while he held her, his head buried in her hair marveling that anyone could make him feel like this.

She was crying in great long sobs now, clinging to him as if he was her savior from the endless heartaches of life. For Sharmila, trained rigorously since the age of twenty-one to suppress all inward and outward expression of real emotion, the relief of letting go was beyond anything she had ever experienced. There had been other men and there had been too many times in the last three years when she had lent her body for Israel but here, tonight, after some of the most harrowing events she had lived through, she had discovered another part of her—a part which belonged not to Israel but to herself alone.

Gently he prized loose her fingers and made her sit down. She refused to raise her head.

Steven Marsh knew he had deliberately changed his whole future and thrown away a set of rules to live by which should have been discarded long ago if he had been honest to himself. The feeling was one of a tremendous burden being lifted from him—a feeling of being free. And it had taken an Israeli girl who he hardly knew less than three days to make him shake off the shackles of a job Marsh realized he had never really wanted. Later he would realize the enormity of what they had let happen but for the moment nothing mattered but Sharmila, the vague disquiet which would come so soon to haunt him as yet unformed in his mind.

She looked up. "It is the same for you?"

Marsh nodded. "If one of us had held on we'd never have known," he said. "You know what we've done, don't you?"

"It's crazy." She made an effort to compose himself.

Marsh didn't want to talk. Nothing had happened but everything had. And he wanted to touch her again.

"What are we going to do?" she whispered.

"Get the hell out of this stinking mess and let the world make out without us. Somewhere inside my head there's an escape plan—I think it's been there for a while but I didn't know before."

She shook her damp hair across her face. "We're a hundred years behind the times. This does not—must not and cannot happen between two people anymore—specially us."

"Sexual attraction," Marsh said, "ordinary biological urge, lust or even personality compatibility. Sure, that's what it's all about for everyone, but the psychologists must've missed out something. We just tripped over it, not even knowing it was there."

She wiped away her tears and smiled. "Shock reaction," she said. "The wish to live at ten times full speed in case we have no tomorrow to look forward to. You didn't mention that one."

"I know all about it and I can taste it now—so can you, but we've been there before and you know damned well it's a wild supercharged feeling, not like this. People never talk about it either."

Sharmila stood up and placed her arms around his neck. "So if we are so special why are we talking?" she whispered to him.

"Because we're frightened it mightn't be real," Marsh answered.

"Only biological urge?" She kissed him.

"Lust," Marsh said, gathering her in his arms and carrying her to the bed. "Maybe there is no tomorrow after all."

"Then love me, Steven."

In a hotel bedroom, far from Israel and far from England, a man and woman let the world rush headlong into another day forgetting for one precious night that for some people there is escape neither from the past nor from reality.

On the floor beside the bed where it had fallen a

crumpled paper envelope waited patiently for the dawn of another morning.

A thousand miles south of Seattle, two men would have willingly exchanged places with Steven Marsh. Had they been able to do so the San Francisco telephone exchange would have been spared the inconvenience of an endless stream of connections and the incredible series of events which they set in motion would never have come to pass.

One of the men was Warren Dahl, sometime head of California's northern division of the CIA—a position which was rapidly becoming untenable and one which Dahl was beginning to wish was not his at all.

Washington had already expressed their displeasure at his inability to reveal the current whereabouts of Sharmila Talmai. Using words which had made Dahl doubt his continued association with the CIA, they had explained that the Jewish embassy was anxious to trace the girl and that as she had been in Dahl's custody a definite answer was expected in the next few hours or sooner.

More recently, the information pouring into his office had caused him to realize that his job might indeed hang upon his performance on what he knew was a project of growing importance. Aware of a serious security leak somewhere inside his organization and with the knowledge that he had allowed Marsh to almost walk out of his hotel, Dahl had resolved to handle the assignment himself.

Some hours had elapsed since he had learned that Marsh and the girl had flown north out of Reno in a rented Cessna. He had also learned of Marsh's earlier flight and of a mysterious package he had left with the man at the airfield. Suspicious of the Englishman ever since he had arrived in California, Dahl was now sure he had been played for a sucker in some way.

Air Traffic Control had confirmed the Cessna's flight

route as heading for the Canadian border also admitting their failure to establish radio contact. Marsh and the girl were running—or had been running for the border, Dahl was sure of that. And they had been carrying a brown paper parcel with them.

Reports from the tiny Reno airstrip had added more to the fast developing story. Seriously beaten up, the operator of the aircraft rental business had told how the Cessna had narrowly avoided being shunted by a car which had chased it furiously up the runway during take-off. Someone was after Marsh or the girl, the same people who had taken them out into the desert? And where did the dead guy the Nevada police had found in the desert fit into all this? Max Navon, a Jew, with enough snake venom in him to kill him ten times over—a connection if ever there was one, Dahl thought, but what the hell was it?

Ninety-two minutes ago—Dahl knew it was ninety-two minutes because he had begun making an event chart to help him keep track of what was happening— ninety-two minutes ago his phone had rung and he had received news of the wreckage of two aircraft on a secondary road east of the Cascade mountains. One of them had been the Cessna.

By this time Warren Dahl had come to the inevitable and unpleasant realization that he was grossly out of his depth. With dark sweat stains on his shirt growing larger with each successive phone call, he began summoning assistance on a scale usually only reserved for assignments of major national importance.

Such was Dahl's anxiety that before sunrise the not inconsiderable facilities of nearly a third of the entire Pacific north-west CIA organization were to be brought into action.

In a different part of San Francisco, seated at the center of a very different but remarkably effective organizational network, another man was also conscious of his failure to complete what he too had originally believed to be a straightforward job. A man of large build who, three days ago, had made the bad mistake of underestimating Steven Marsh and the young Jewish girl when they had given him the slip in the Nevada desert.

For the sum of one hundred thousand dollars he had guaranteed delivery of a set of drawings to an address in Salt Lake City. He had infiltrated the CIA with little difficulty. He had learned of the CIA's plans to intercept his helicopter and only by accident had his recovery system foundered at the last moment. Later, he had successfully located the Englishman, led to him by the girl who he now knew must have escaped from the wrecked Cessna together with Marsh.

Behind a plain wooden desk in his temporary Berkeley office he sat deep in thought, the room lit by a solitary naked bulb hanging from the ceiling.

Eight dead men. One in the helicopter, two in the Chevrolet—gunned down by another of his men who had also died. Then the wasted attempt to extract information from the Englishman using the snake—yet another of his men dead unnecessarily. And now three others incinerated in the remains of their Beech aircraft. In terms of lives, the cost had already been enormous, but he was not a man given to sympathy and, because of the incompetence of others, he knew now it was necessary for him to finish the job alone. Like Warren Dahl, he too had decided that he would have to handle matters by himself.

Reaching out for the telephone in front of him, he dialed a local number.

"This is Edward Cabinda," he said. "I am leaving for Tacoma immediately. For the time being you will continue to act as co-ordinator and I therefore expect you to have located Marsh and the girl by the time I call you again. You have my authority to use the remainder of the funds you hold if it proves necessary.

Providing you have the information I require when I telephone you from Tacoma, we will not meet again. If you do not have the information you know what to expect. I trust these instructions are clear to you?" He listened for a moment before replacing the receiver.

From the breast pocket of his expensive suit he withdrew a business card on which was printed a single seven digit number. Placing it carefully in the center of the desk he considered the risk of committing himself to a final delivery date. If he failed this time it would be more than his reputation which would suffer. The terms of his contract were specific in the extreme and one more mistake would be one too many.

Almost reluctantly he reached for the phone again.

"I wish to make a person to person call to London," he said quietly.

Whilst the telephone lines of San Francisco carried their messages swiftly out across the United States and to more distant places, other events of equal significance were taking place in two other countries.

From his home in Jerusalem, using data supplied by the Israeli embassy in London, Colonel Yaacobi was engaged in the organization of a bold plan to locate agents Steven Marsh and Sharmila Talmai. His arrangements were abruptly curtailed by the news of yet another Palestinian guerrilla attack in a crowded Tel Aviv street. Fourteen Israeli civilians had died before Yaacobi put his phone down.

In London, John Reylord had been instructed to report to the U.K. Foreign Office for urgent discussions with a gentleman representing British Intelligence. At the same time, also in London, the president of the Federation of Anglo-American Companies had received a message of such importance that he found it necessary to interrupt birthday celebrations for his wife in order to travel to Heathrow air terminal as fast as his Rolls would carry him. All across the northern hemisphere, from the west coast of America to Israel, the hunt for the Kfir missile drawings had intensified to a degree which could not have been foreseen by any of the people involved. Had any of them known of the others' intentions, the situation which was about to occur could perhaps have been avoided.

CHAPTER TWELVE

Following the passage of the water trucks during the night, a brief shower of rain had scoured what remained of the dirt from Seattle's streets.

From the hotel bedroom high above Fifth Avenue, the slick of water covering the sidewalk gave the whole street the appearance of being polished.

Marsh withdrew his head from the window and began to examine his clothes. Dusty and badly torn in a couple of places he was surprised he had experienced so little difficulty in checking into the hotel last night.

He pulled on his trousers then caught sight of himself in the mirror.

A fresh bruise four inches in diameter was superimposed on his old scar, the slash of white piercing the purple area like a surrealist painting of the planet Saturn. Running horizontally across his stomach the line of stitches he had received in the Las Vegas hospital added to the disfigurement. A scarred body, he thought, one which had served him well enough in the past and one which was due for a long rest. The face staring back at him was even more gaunt than usual, lines at the corners of his eyes seeming more like creases now he came to look at them more closely.

He swore at his own reflection, effectively ripping himself out of the mood he had lapsed into. There was much to do and time was against them. A whole night had been squandered, a night in which Steven Marsh, agent of British Intelligence, had become Steven Marsh, man on the run.

His bare foot touched the parcel on the floor. Picking it up, holding it as though the tattered brown paper wrapping conained all that he wished to forget of the past, he wondered what they were going to do with it.

The dream he had lived for such a short while began to slip through the fingers which held the drawings. Gradually he felt his vision of happiness drain away.

Placing the package on the bed he turned to face Sharmila as she came out of the bathroom. Her face dropped as she saw his expression.

"What is it?" she asked anxiously. "Steven, tell me —now what's wrong?"

He shook his head. "Nothing, I just wish it was last night again."

She saw the parcel. "That's the trouble, isn't it?"

"It's a bad start," he admitted. "I suppose you want to mail it to Israel?"

She came close to him. "It doesn't belong to anyone else, but I didn't say that. We'll decide together. Please don't talk about it now."

"You can't pretend it doesn't exist," he said. But he knew she was right. To stupidly force the issue now could destroy everything.

Rising on to her toes she wound her arms around his neck and kissed him full on the mouth. "Seychelles," she whispered. "We have a long way to go— we had better start as soon as we can."

For a second she recaptured the dream for him. Such was her magic that in one simple direct action she could change his whole thought pattern. He made himself forget what had gone before, lifting her from the floor in a long embrace. When he lowered her again, morning sunshine had returned to the room.

"Seychelles," he agreed. "Us. And to hell with everything else. That bloody parcel is coming with us for insurance, but that's all. First, Miss Talmai, we make Canada—then we're on our way properly."

She began collecting the few clothes they had not yet put on.

Marsh took his shirt away from her. "Stop fussing," he said. "Just get ready—we're leaving straight away. Like you said we've got a long way to go."

"It doesn't seem right," she said. "We're starting out with nothing—nothing at all."

"We never had anything," Marsh answered. "A gun, an expense account and maybe a cause—a crusade even for you. I didn't even have one of those."

She smiled at him. "You mean we've traded all those things just for each other?"

He shook his head and reached into his hip pocket producing a wad of money.

"You've forgotten your dowry. We've got about five hundred dollars left. It's plenty for a start and I've got enough friends scattered around the world to make sure we don't come to a grinding halt halfway there. You ready?"

"I was ready two days ago—you didn't know though."

Stopping before he reached the door Marsh turned round. "You can't fool me, two days ago Israel was still more important—come on, brown eyes."

She took a few steps towards him. "Israel has always been important—I'm not running out on my country. Don't be so arrogant—I'm not exchanging Israel for you. I've just decided I can't do without you, that's all." She took his hand in a familiar gesture. "All you have to do is believe in me and take me with you."

Three minutes later, they were out on the sidewalk on a fresh September morning ready to begin something which neither of them had believed could ever begin. No commuter traffic had yet arrived to spoil the quiet emptiness of the streets, only the odd car squealing its tires as it accelerated away from the numerous sets of traffic lights spanning the length of Fifth Avenue. It was a good morning on which to start again.

Walking downhill in the direction of the waterfront they soon crossed Fourth Avenue, steadily moving away from the more expensive part of town. Gradually they were joined by more people appearing from nowhere to hurry on their way to jobs in one of Seattle's less elegant neighborhoods.

Pausing at the next intersection, Marsh steered her into a small café already full of noisy activity. Several heads turned as Sharmila accompanied him to the counter. He wasn't sure if he liked it or not.

"Pancakes and coffee," Marsh said, "and two packets of Chesterfield, please."

They ate in silence, devouring four enormous pancakes each before Marsh sat back to light a cigarette.

"I'm still hungry, Steven." She looked at him pleadingly.

"You can't be, it's impossible," he said. "No one could manage more than four let alone someone your size."

"I need building up."

Nothing, Marsh thought, could be further from the truth, the open glances of admiration she was receiving from the predominantly male occupants of the restaurant serving only to reinforce his opinion. He paid the bill ignoring her protests.

Out in the street again, feeling very much better, he started searching for one of those shops which deal exclusively in good quality working clothes. They found two, neither of them yet open for business.

To pass the time he took Sharmila for a leisurely tour of First Avenue. Here the water trucks seemed to have neglected their work, beer cans and newspapers from the night still littering the street. Part of the street has a reputation of being a living graveyard for Seattle's less successful residents but it was an area

Marsh knew relatively well. And he knew its appearance concealed places where some very clever people had established unusual and extraordinarily profitable businesses.

At the door of one of them he stopped to inspect a number of white cards held in place beneath a grimy sheet of glass.

"A bit more insurance," he explained to Sharmila, placing his finger on a brass bell push.

"I'm coming in with you," she said suddenly. "You didn't want me to wait here, did you?"

"No," Marsh said. "I'm a funny guy. Once I've made up my mind that's it. From now on I want you around all the time." He grinned at her. "This'll only take a minute."

In fact it was nearly half an hour before they managed to escape the clutches of the owner of the card. Greeting Marsh as an old friend, which indeed he was, the wealthy Jewish businessman who operated from these unimpressive premises was delighted to hear that Sharmila had recently arrived in the States from Israel. Eager to learn first hand of Israel's recent fortunes and to catch up on the latest political news, it proved extremely difficult for her to stop the flood of questions.

The transaction which Marsh eventually completed cost him a cool hundred and twenty dollars but he was not displeased with his purchases. In a second-hand but comparatively smart pigskin suitcase, thrown into the deal for nothing, he carried two items of equipment which he hoped fervently would become no more than unused momentoes of an uneventful run for freedom.

The first of these was a Universal .30 caliber M1 semi-automatic pistol, the second a finely made Italian flick knife with a blade ground from Swedish steel. Sharmila had chosen it for herself.

For long enough Marsh had been forced to operate relying on nothing but his wits. Now, in circumstances of a very different kind, Steven Marsh was not going to be stopped. Once again he was equipped with teeth.

Back at the clothing store they spent ten busy minutes in outfitting themselves with serviceable jeans and a warm jacket each. Storing their old things in the suitcase, it was a very different couple who emerged from the doorway to join the rapidly growing crowds filling the streets on this sunny morning.

In order to minimize the risk of further trouble and to give them breathing space, Marsh had decided upon a slightly unconventional method of traveling the last hundred and fifty miles to Canada. Although he knew they would be only marginally safer once they had left America, experience had shown him that, as an Englishman, operating inside Canada was very much easier than in the States and his contacts in Vancouver were also surprisingly extensive. Some years ago, two jobs in the Pacific north-west—one of them lasting nearly three months—had allowed Marsh to explore much of this part of the world. As a precaution he had taken care to keep in touch with some of the more useful people he had met, for in Marsh's business, contacts to be trusted could mean the difference between success and failure, even life or death if you were unlucky.

On this occasion he intended to use Vancouver as a springboard to a new life and his friends there could help him make sure he made a foolproof take-off—a take-off which would leave no telltale pointers behind.

Spotting a taxi in the distance Marsh stepped off the sidewalk to make quite sure the driver could not miss him. In this locality and at this time of morning, empty taxis were far from plentiful and Marsh was anxious to begin the next part of their trip without further delay.

The car drew to a halt on the other side of the road then executed a sharp U-turn to pull up with its front bumper only inches from Marsh's legs. He grinned through the windshield at the large black driver before walking round to speak to him through the open window.

"We'd like to go to Fisherman's Terminal in Salmon Bay," Marsh said, "and that means you're facing the wrong way."

The driver returned the grin. "Man, if that's going to be the biggest problem of the day, she's going to be a sweet one." He leaned back to open the rear door.

Marsh placed the suitcase on the floor and climbed in after Sharmila. He waited until the driver had made another equally rapid turn before lighting a cigarette and settling back in his seat.

Although there was already plenty of warmth in the sun, Sharmila had elected to wear her new jacket. Beneath it, her white blouse was open at the neck revealing the gentle swell of her breasts and Marsh could see one of the savage bruises she had received when the Cessna had crashed. For a moment he wondered if fate was going to allow them to escape so easily.

Since they had first met at the Las Vegas motel they had been attended by nothing but violence in one form or another and again it occurred to him that he was perhaps being stupid in believing it was possible to disappear when so many important people were vitally interested in finding out where they were.

He sat watching the buildings drift by the window, letting his mind explore some of the ways which could rid them of pursuit. Israel, the United States Government, the British, and cruel violent men representing the companies which had stolen the drawings—all prepared to expend whatever was necessary in terms of dollars or lives to secure the slim package in the suitcase alongside his feet. If hurling it out of the window could have solved the problem Marsh would willingly have done just that. But no matter how attractive the idea seemed he knew that in reality its disposal would solve nothing. A more daring plan was needed and, if he failed to think of one, total disappearance into obscurity was all that was left if he was to have any sort of life with Sharmila. He glanced at her again as if to remind him of what he was doing.

She sensed his interest, turning her head to look him in the eyes.

"Do I pass?" she asked. "Sometimes I know what you're thinking."

"I can't help wondering what our friends are up to —that doesn't mean I'm having second thoughts though. I've already told you—I've made up my mind."

"And you don't worry about me changing my mind?"

"No," Marsh said. "Should I?"

She shook her head slightly. "No, never. Not ever."

Turning sharply from West Emerson, a forest of white masts appeared directly ahead. The driver nosed his car into a crowded parking area and twisted round in his seat. "This okay?"

"Fine, thanks," Marsh replied, passing a note. "Keep the change. Maybe today'll turn out to be pretty good after all."

Sharmila handed Marsh the case before sliding out of the taxi. She stood beside him as it moved away.

A hundred and fifty yards behind them from a partly open window in an unobtrusive and run-down warehouse, a patient man lifted his pair of binoculars to inspect the people the taxi had delivered.

As they walked slowly away from him in the direction of the wharf he reached for his telephone to check on what he had seen and to obtain new instructions. Already the sensitive tip of one long probing CIA tentacle had touched something it recognized.

Had Marsh known they had been located there would still have been time to change his plan—make a run for it and perhaps elude the network which had been set up to catch them. But he could not know that Warren Dahl had stationed men at every conceivable port of departure and as he approached the waterfront he was pleased with his idea of using Puget Sound as a method of crossing America's border with Canada.

With mooring capacity for a thousand craft, Fisherman's Terminal this morning seemed so packed with vessels that Marsh had some difficulty in deciding where to begin his search.

Many of the fishing boats showed no obvious signs of being occupied whilst others were in the last stages of making ready to leave. The characteristic smell of diesel fumes and stale fish hung heavily in the air, the atmosphere reminding him more of Europe than North America.

For nearly five minutes they wandered back and forth along piers between the closely grouped boats nodding to numerous sunburned faces which appeared from cabin hatches at the sound of feet. Then, three-quarters of the way along the fifth pier, Marsh saw what he was looking for. Not a boat, but a combination of boat and captain.

Sitting idly on a cabin top a young man had caught sight of Sharmila. Not wishing to stare yet reluctant to allow her to pass by before he had confirmed his first impression, he overcame the dilemma by shouting a hearty good morning and waving his hand.

Leaving Sharmila to entertain the owner which she accomplished simply by standing still and smiling, Marsh quickly cast his eye over the launch. A little over forty feet long, it was not, and never had been, a pure fishing boat. Perhaps twenty years old and freshly painted it had the lines of an old game fishing launch, the cabin appearing to have been added in stages by a number of different owners having no feeling for beauty or line.

"Where would I find the launch *Bremerton?*" Marsh shouted, using the first local name which entered his head.

The young man slid down on to the deck and came

over to talk. "Never heard of her," he said. "Nearly all trawlers here, though. You're in the wrong place for launches."

Dressed in faded jeans and an extensively patched denim jacket, the captain or deck hand would be in his early twenties, Marsh thought. Something told him he had hit pay dirt at his first attempt.

"I was told I could find the *Bremerton* here," he said. "I'm sure the guy said Fisherman's Terminal."

Sharmila was sure too. "That's right," she said. "We'd better go on looking, she'll be here somewhere." She addressed the young man directly. "Could you give us any idea where we might find any other boats like yours?"

He shook his head thoughtfully. "Can't say as I can but if it's fishing you're after the old *Tahuya* here is all ready to go." He saw the suitcase in Marsh's hand and decided he'd misinterpreted the situation. "Or if you're looking for a few days up in the San Juans—" He finished lamely as if embarrassed to be canvassing for trade so blatantly.

"Your own boat?" Marsh inquired.

"Will be in a couple of years. Then I'll get a better one."

Marsh eyed the hull. "If she was mine and if she's as sound as she looks I'd rip off everything above deck level and build a real nice cabin to match the rest of her."

The owner of the *Tahuya* was not to be drawn into a discussion on the merits of his launch. Instead he seemed to see through the somewhat thin attempt Marsh had made to engage him in conversation. "Twenty-five dollars an hour," he said bluntly.

"Twenty and no questions," Marsh replied equally bluntly.

"If you've got drugs in that case, try somewhere else."

"We haven't," Sharmila said. "Do we look the sort of people?"

"Show me"—the young man reached out a hand. All embarrassment had gone.

Marsh made no effort to pass it to him. "Twenty an hour and we start now if there're no drugs?"

"Where to?"

"North," Marsh answered. "Can we come aboard?" He tossed the case casually on to the deck hoping he was not making a mistake.

Springing lightly from the pier on to the bow of the launch he held out a hand to help Sharmila cross the narrow gap of water. She ignored his offer of assistance, jumped easily to join him then knelt down beside the young man as he withdrew the semi-automatic pistol.

"No drugs," she said sweetly, taking it from his hands and replacing it in the case. "And no questions, remember? My name is Gina, what's yours?"

He rose to his feet and stuck out his hand. "Jay Lynd and I'm pleased to meet you Gina. I'm probably mad—but okay, no questions."

"Murray Stacks," Marsh introduced himself. He picked up the case. "I'll cast off for you if I could put this inside somewhere."

Lynd looked him squarely in the eyes. "Five hours' down payment seem unreasonable?"

Marsh grinned. "No, it doesn't," he peeled off a hundred dollars and gave it to him. "You got a thing about dope?"

"My sister," Lynd replied shortly. "I don't much like guns either, Mr. Stacks, but I guess I'm old-fashioned. Put your case in the wheelhouse. You can let go the forward warp right away—I'll tell you when I'm ready for the one aft."

Whilst the *Tahuya* made ready her departure, a few miles south of Fisherman's Terminal, another launch was also preparing to leave her berth. By the time Jay

Lynd had navigated the short reaches of Salmon Bay and turned his bows north into Puget Sound, a full description of his boat had been radioed to the captain of the other vessel.

And in Tacoma, a man called Edward Cabinda was quietly congratulating himself on the efficiency of his own arrangements. Despite the tightest security the CIA could manage, no sooner had the CIA telephones in San Francisco begun to carry messages back to Seattle than other lines of communication were brought into play. Although he did not know it, Warren Dahl had been betrayed again and this time there would be no second chance.

So it was that the launch *Tahuya* left the mainland carrying an Englishman, a young Jewish girl and a much traveled and battered set of drawings defining the manner in which a missile homing system could be built.

A fine September morning for two people to escape from lives they had decided were no longer relevant and a fine morning to travel through the soft greenness of the San Juan islands which stretched ahead of them.

With water creaming from her bow, the *Tahuya* increased her speed to fifteen knots leaving a rippled wake to wash away the past of her Canadian bound passengers. But the ripples would not be allowed to die down and vanish into the tranquillity of the Sound. Instead they formed the white feathered end of a long arrow pointing its sharpened barbs at the unsuspecting backs of Steven Marsh and the girl he loved.

CHAPTER THIRTEEN

In late summer, Puget Sound is an enchanting inland sea much favored by tourists from all over the States and used extensively by the pleasure boating fraternity which has grown up along its eastern shoreline.

To the west the Olympic mountains form a huge barrier to the Pacific, creating a majestic backdrop to the San Juan islands dotted haphazardly between Vancouver island and the north-west coast of the Washington mainland. With the exception of weekends it is still a silent uncrowded part of America.

This morning only a small number of craft were heading north, most of the boats which the *Tahuya* encountered either being anchored or drifting with the tide whilst their occupants sat lazily in the sunshine waiting for a tug on their fishing lines to wake them from their daydreaming.

Ahead of *Tahuya* the Victoria bound ferry was pushing its blunt bows through the water to cause the only real disturbance to the placid Sound as far as the eye could see. A peaceful scene and one typical enough for this hour on a weekday.

Lost in his own thoughts, Steven Marsh stood motionless in the bow of the launch. Using one hand to steady himself against the occasional pitch generated by the wake of the ferry, he was enjoying the breeze whilst he tried to remember the names of the islands they would pass. The sea air and the freshness of the environment was adding to the sense of freedom he had been experiencing since they had left the hotel. He turned round to see if Sharmila had yet lost the expression of delight she had been wearing for the last hour or so.

Sitting cross-legged on the cabin top her long hair streaming out behind her she laughed as he nearly overbalanced.

"Come on up here," he shouted.

She shook her head and pointed to a lone seagull which was overtaking them without any obvious sign of effort. Marsh watched it soar past. Bound for Canada perhaps or wherever the wind currents or its fancy took it. Freedom of the purest kind, he thought, something that man could no longer achieve.

Jay Lynd had left the wheelhouse to come forward. He stood beside Marsh noticing a strange longing in the eyes of the passenger.

"If there's anything you want to tell me," he said, "now might be a good time."

Marsh remained staring at the gull until it disappeared into the distance. "It's one hell of a long story," he said, "and I wouldn't know where to start. You'll have to make do with a happy ending. This is it—or the start of it."

"Maybe you should postpone things, Mr. Stacks. Like I said, if there's anything I should know it could help. We're being followed by a police launch."

Marsh turned to look at him then directed his gaze to the rear. A mile astern of the *Tahuya,* the westernmost tip of Whidbey island was blocking his view of any vessel which could be shadowing them.

"You're sure?" he asked, unwilling to believe his dream could be shattered by a young man's simple statement. Then one by one Marsh felt his old senses awaken. The tightening of the guts, a hint of dryness in his throat and the stirring of a tired but still sharp awareness which had served him so well over the years. Slowly a bitter resentment rose within him, completing the transformation. For less than twenty-four hours he had been allowed to be the new man he had promised Sharmila—now after so little time he was back where he had been so many times before.

Jay Lynd had watched the change take place. "No, I'm not sure," he said quietly. "But if it's not following us the skipper's doing a real good imitation of it. She's been behind for three hours and gaining slowly. I'm guessing they were expecting us to head for Victoria and would've come alongside just before we crossed into Canadian waters. Now they're waiting to see where we're going." He pushed his hands into his pockets. "If I'm right, that is."

"How far behind?" Marsh asked, his voice steady.

"Mile and a half, two miles maybe. They'd reckon on being able to catch the old *Tahuya* up with a quick burst." He smiled broadly at Marsh. "They must have forgotten."

"And you think I'd be interested in the fact that we're being followed by the police?" Marsh said.

Lynd's smile remained. "I know you are."

"What have the Seattle police forgotten?"

"Come on back to the wheelhouse," Lynd said. You'd better get her off there, too," he nodded at Sharmila. "You don't have to explain, Mr. Stacks. If I let the cops come on board and if by any chance at all you're in trouble of some kind then I'm in trouble as well as you. There's an easier way."

"Sharmila," Marsh shouted. "Come on down a minute."

As before she shook her head.

"Look behind," Marsh pointed to the red and white launch rounding the island promontory in the distance.

She slid down immediately and joined them in the cabin, a puzzled look on her face. Marsh stopped her from asking questions.

"Why?" he said to Lynd. "Why help us?"

"Just so as you don't think I'm more stupid than I

really am—two reasons. One, I have no time for the bastards in that boat. Two, as I said, they wouldn't believe you chartered the *Tahuya*—they'd throw me in with the mess you're in, whatever it is—I've been here before, Mr. Stacks, and I know how it is. Is that enough?"

"No," Marsh said, "but it doesn't matter. I still want to know what they've forgotten."

Lynd bent down and opened a small hatch in the deck to expose a neat instrument panel. "Two years ago this was my father's launch. He used to do a regular run between Canada and the States carrying enough stuff to make a living—even did the odd bit of smuggling. The police found half a pound of heroin inside a box of frozen salmon someone had asked him to drop off in Vancouver—my old man didn't stand a chance." He pulled a black knob on the panel and flipped a switch.

At once, from deep in the bowels of the *Tahuya*, a throbbing growl confirmed what Marsh had already half-suspected.

"What about your sister, Jay?" Sharmila asked.

Lynd straightened. "Got hooked in high school," he said shortly. "The cops said my father had got the stuff for her. He wasn't even going the right way."

"How fast can we go?" Marsh asked him.

"On a flat sea like this—forty-six knots. That's about sixteen more than the cops can manage."

Marsh could not conceal his surprise.

Noticing his expression Lynd prepared to demonstrate. "Before the noise starts we'd better decide where I'm going to dump you."

"It'd better not be too far away," Marsh said. "Soon as they see us take off they'll radio ahead."

"Sometimes," Sharmila said, "sometimes I think we'll never ever get to Canada. It's not even very far but I'm beginning to believe we'll never make it."

Marsh put his arm round her waist. "Yes we will.

Every time we get a bit closer." He turned to inspect the map Lynd had spread out on the chart table.

The young man pointed to the northern tip of Whidbey island. "Anacortes," he said. "There's a road to the mainland from there—takes you into Burlington."

Marsh was thinking. "If we carry on at this speed," he said, "they won't be expecting us to try anything clever. Just as we clear the end of the island you turn right then give it everything you've got and drop us here"—he indicated a small wharf marked on the chart. "Then you turn round, go like hell back to where you were and throttle back. By the time you get there they'll never know you diverted for five minutes. They won't have seen anything."

Lynd grinned. "I might lead them a dance up through the islands—you never know I might get them to rip their insides out on a couple of rocks my Dad showed me."

"You don't think they'll have anyone standing by at Anacortes?" Sharmila asked. "Someone must have seen us leave Seattle." Her face showed concern and like Marsh she too was in the process of losing her grip on their dream.

"We wouldn't have hired the *Tahuya* to take us to Anacortes," Marsh replied. "We'll be okay there. Anyway we haven't got much choice."

"I'll have to let them catch me in the end," Lynd said. "They'll only nail me when I get back otherwise. I'll tell them I was just out for a run—alone."

"They're still catching us up," Sharmila observed, looking over her shoulder.

Lynd glanced at the launch now only about a mile behind.

"No problem," he said. "We'll do what Mr. Stacks says. Half an hour from now you'll see the old *Tahuya* climb clear out of the water." He used the tip of his sandshoe to switch off the second engine. "Save our fuel until we're ready."

"Hell, I'm sorry," Marsh said. "But thanks for helping us out, anyway." He placed a sheaf of dollars on the table beside the chart.

Lynd picked them up and handed them back to him. "I figure you'll need these more than I will—you keep it."

Marsh smiled and returned the money to his pocket.

"You don't want to tell me the story?" Lynd could not resist the question.

Sharmila answered him. "The police will try and get information from you—"

The young American interrupted her. "And if I know nothing then nothing's all they'll get. Okay, send me a postcard, though."

Once the ferry had been overtaken and left astern, for the rest of the journey along the shoreline of the narrow island the three people on board the *Tahuya* spent most of the remaining minutes watching the police launch draw steadily closer. Marsh made a number of careful calculations checking the distance Lynd would have to travel once they rounded the end of the island, finally suggesting it was necessary to increase their speed very slightly to guarantee success of the maneuver.

Soon it was time to begin. Lynd restarted the powerful motor, letting it idle for some minutes before sticking out his hand to say good-bye. "Nice meeting you —luck. There won't be time later."

Marsh wished there was something he could say and was grateful when Sharmila did it for him. Taking Lynd's hand in both of her own she held it for a long time before turning away.

"Better grab something," Lynd advised. Leaning forward he pulled back on a polished brass lever.

Immediately the growl of the engines turned into a deep roar and the bows of the *Tahuya* began to rise. Higher and higher they lifted until the launch lay at an impossible angle with her stern nearly submerged in boiling water. Then, as the engine peaked, she surged forward. Barely touching the surface in the closest thing to level flight Marsh had experienced in a large power-boat, the launch dropped to a horizontal position as it accelerated to its maximum speed.

With the whole fabric of the hull vibrating from the two enormous engines and the slightest ripple on the water sending hammer blows upwards to the deck, Marsh was conscious of an exhilaration that only swift travel over water can achieve.

All too quickly the outskirts of Anacortes appeared on the starboard bow.

In a long graceful curve of white foam Lynd brought them through an obstacle course of moored boats without reducing speed.

Sharmila had a hand over her mouth as they hurtled towards the wharf. At the last minute Lynd shoved his lever forward. A tremendous cloud of spray fountained upwards over the wheelhouse as the launch sank back to its waterline, the suddenness of the stop taking both disembarking passengers by surprise.

Together Marsh and Sharmila scrambled along the pitching deck, jumping side by side on to a rickety wooden landing stage as the *Tahuya* wallowed by, caught by her own stern wave which curled up and over the transom.

Marsh raised a hand in farewell, his shout of thanks drowned by the renewed howl from the exhaust. In his other hand he held the suitcase.

Again Lynd nagivated his way through the rows of bobbing boats avoiding using full power until he was well clear of them. Then there was a quick wave from him before the rooster tail hid him from view.

A noticeable glow of excitement had flushed Sharmila's cheeks. "We should have gone all the way like that," she said. "In the Seychelles we'll have a fast boat, too."

"It's a long way," Marsh smiled. "We'd better start

walking or it'll be dark before we get there." Taking
her hand he set off down one of the narrow streets leading away from the wharf.

Had he taken the trouble to use his eyes he would
have realized the Seychelles were moving further away
with each step forward.

Two hundred yards away on board an expensive
cruiser, with a twisted smile on his face, Edward Cabinda thought that the Gods had indeed been kind. To
have been spared a journey by the vessel he had recently chartered was one thing. For Marsh and the girl
to walk straight into his hands was quite another.

The idea of them landing here in Anacortes had
understandably not occurred to him and, throughout
his car journey up here from Tacoma, he had been
anticipating difficulty in continuing his pursuit by water.

Now the arrangements he had just concluded with
the captain of the cruiser were redundant. Now he could
finish his business with the minimum of inconvenience.

The pigskin suitcase Marsh was carrying had not
escaped his attention nor had the fact that the Englishman appeared totally at ease despite his somewhat spectacular and unexpected arrival at the waterfront.

A remarkable coincidence, Cabinda thought, an opportunity to seize the drawings almost without effort.
And this time there would be no mistakes and this
time he would not underestimate the ability of the two
people who had caused him so much trouble. Taking
care to remain out of sight he made his way back to
his car.

Although Marsh may have given his observer the
impression of being particularly relaxed, he had been
thinking of the comment Sharmila had made. Because
of it he had already begun searching the waterfront for
any unusual sign of activity.

"Dahl could have stationed someone here, too," he
said. "Salmon Bay wasn't exactly the most obvious

place for us to have made for." He stopped walking whilst he lit a cigarette.

"No, but the CIA wouldn't expect us to use roads," Sharmila replied. "Why have they decided we're trying to get to Canada?"

"I don't know—maybe we shouldn't be," Marsh sounded tired. "Can you see anything we should've seen five minutes ago?"

She shook her head. "I can get us out of this," she said staring at the ground. "One long distance phone call."

"So can I. I'd guess I could have a Canadian boat here in a few hours. Even Israel couldn't do that. Do we toss for who phones who, exchange the drawings for a free trip to London or Jerusalem and then go on from there?"

"Why not, as long as we don't fight over the decision." She began walking again then swung round to face him. "What does it matter, Steven—nothing has changed, has it?"

A highly-polished gray Ford was traveling towards them from the direction of the waterfront. Inside it the driver gripped the checkered handle of his silenced Colt automatic, his eyes fixed on the two people talking on the sidewalk.

What happened next was a combination of two things. The fact that Sharmila was able to see the car the instant it appeared and her exceptional eyesight.

It took her perhaps five full seconds to recognize the large man behind the wheel. By then it was too late.

Seeing the expression of horror on her face, Marsh turned.

"Down there," he yelled pointing at an alleyway on the opposite side of the road.

Realizing he had been spotted, Cabinda floored his accelerator bearing down on his victims as they sprinted across the street.

The front fender of the Ford missed Marsh by inches, leaving him to vanish temporarily into the alley.

Hauling the Tee-bar on his automatic into reverse, Cabinda overshot by less than twenty feet. Tires smoking he brought the car back, his gun ready at the open window.

Leaving the engine running he strained his eyes in an attempt to penetrate the dark shadows thrown by the buildings lining the garbage-strewn lane to his right.

Any further escape effectively prevented by a high wooden fence, Steven Marsh and Sharmila Talmai crouched, hearts beating, behind a group of rusty trash cans watching the man in the car.

Marsh had already abandoned the suitcase, leaving Sharmila to carry the packet of drawings whilst he fumbled with the magazine on his M1 automatic.

In bright sunshine, at a range of thirty yards, the driver made an attractive target but Marsh knew that one shot from his gun would bring half of Anacortes here. Holding the M1 in both hands as if it were a machine-pistol he waited. Beside him Sharmila had stuffed the drawings into a pocket of her jacket. Marsh heard the click of her knife opening.

Aware that he was vulnerable in his present postion, Cabinda moved the Ford forward, switched off the ignition and got out. The quiet back street was deserted.

Cautiously he approached the mouth of the alley ready with his gun. Gradually his eyes adjusted to the shadows allowing him to confirm his first impression. Unless they had disappeared through one of the many doors lining the alley they could be only in one place.

There was a noise from his gun like a baseball bat squashing a ripe pumpkin.

Firing from the hip, Cabinda had given Marsh no warning of his intention. The bullet smacked through both walls of the can in front of Sharmila passing dangerously close to her face.

Although unwilling to reveal their presence Marsh

knew he had no other choice. Another exploratory shot from the man who was here to search them out could easily prove fatal.

Raising the M1 Marsh squeezed the trigger twice. In the narrow confines of the alleyway the noise was ear-splitting. Two long white slivers of wood flew from the far corner of the building in the distance but he was unfamiliar with his weapon and the shots were wide.

Trapped like rats in the end of a closed drain, Marsh thought, Christ what a way for it all to end. He stood up, the alley appearing in stark black and white to him as he waited for the next act. No fear, no desire to kill his adversary—nothing but resentment. Fate had been unnecessarily cruel. Why couldn't he have met her a year ago? A month ago even—days were not enough. Still he waited knowing there were only seconds left.

Fully exposed to the eyes of anyone passing along the street, Cabinda was painfully aware of the tremendous noise from Marsh's gun. At any moment Anacortes was going to wake up. Marsh had assessed the situation perfectly and Cabinda knew time was running out. He began to ease himself round the corner.

Three more shots rang out followed by the sound of splintering wood.

Cabinda sprang forwards, his gun spitting silently at the figure which seemed to be rebounding from one wall.

The heavy .45 slug smashed horribly into the soft flesh under Marsh's right arm hurling him to the ground.

Paralyzed with the pain his grip relaxed. The M1 skittered away from him to crash into the garbage cans.

Swinging open crookedly on its hinges, the door he had smashed open with two bullets and his shoulder was making a creaking sound. There was still time for her.

"Go on," he shouted desperately, "Sharmila, go on!"

It was her own flying figure that saved Marsh from another bullet and certain death.

Leaping from her hiding place, she crossed the alley in one spurt throwing herself through the gap as the second of Cabinda's shots ricocheted off the stone portal.

Simultaneously the wail of a police siren sounded a few blocks away.

"Steven!"—she held out her hands to him.

"Run!" Marsh shouted. "Never mind me—go!" He tensed himself for the final bullet, seeing her face distorted as he tried to roll himself towards the inadequate protection offered by the gutter.

Tires squealed in the distance and the siren was much louder.

He tried to smile at her. The agony in her eyes was terrible. She stepped back into the darkness of the building and suddenly was gone.

Cabinda was struggling with his own decisions.

Two elderly men had appeared from a nearby timber store and the gunshots would undoubtedly attract others stupid enough to come out on the street.

In an almost suicidal slide, an Anacortes police car rocketed round the corner bouncing violently over the curb as the driver struggled for control.

For a second Cabinda was tempted to stay and fight. Then he ran heavily to his car. Cursing his misfortune, convinced he had lost everything, he started the engine and rammed the shift lever into drive.

As the Ford began to move he reached out to slam the door.

Propelled by a fury which carried her to the car in one headlong rush, Sharmila burst from the front door of the warehouse.

Her knife carved deeply into his shoulder as he tried vainly to fend off the hellcat who had sprung at him. Clawing her way inside the car, Sharmila raised her blade and stabbed out viciously again.

Still gaining speed, the Ford reached forty-five miles an hour with Cabinda fighting for his life with his free hand. Bleeding profusely from an unknown number of cuts, he had so far managed to escape a fatal wound but was surviving only by using his fist and bloody forearm as a club.

The knife plunged into the top of his seat allowing him to seize the upper hand as she struggled to free it.

Grabbing her hair he wrenched her head down and using all his strength tipped her bodily into the back of the Ford. Like an enraged animal Sharmila surfaced to renew her attack.

There was no time and Cabinda was a callous man.

Straightening the wheel he held it momentarily with his knee. He snatched his gun from the floor where it had fallen and swiveled round.

At a range of three feet, as the girl came at him again, he pulled the trigger.

Cabinda could elude the Anacortes police and perhaps the game was not yet totally lost after all. Hunched over the wheel he slid the Ford out of the township on to a faster road wondering where they'd put the first road block.

Not long from now Edward Cabinda would discover that his Gods had been kinder than he thought. On the back seat of his car, in the blood soaked jacket of the girl, the Kfir missile drawings were on yet another leg of their tragic journey.

CHAPTER FOURTEEN

Although the venue had been chosen with care and although a general air of informality seemed to fill the large room, each person at the meeting was acutely conscious of a suppressed tension which was growing with each new arrival.

Chain smoking at one end of the room John Reylord stood alone staring out at the lawn through the open window.

Bearing the flag of the United States on its gleaming front mudguard yet another car drew up at the wide stone steps leading to the front door. He watched the American ambassador get out accompanied by a man whom he had met once before somewhere. Reylord tried to recall where. The names of some of the men already grouped round the table were known to him but they were unimportant names and as the meeting would consist of those who would do the talking and those who would listen, he had concerned himself only with remembering the names of the men who would contribute to the final decision. He turned round to meet the ambassador wondering if it would prove necessary to remember the name of the man who was with him.

Warren Dahl was openly introduced to Reylord as a senior member of the CIA, the ambassador thus making it quite clear to both men that Dahl's association with the agency would soon be over.

Reylord shook hands with him, glad that the CIA had

made such a bloody mess of things. He was equally pleased with the lack of success which the British had experienced. Secure in the knowledge that he could now not be involved in any secret double-cross which the British or Americans had planned, John Reylord felt confident of his ability to rationalize the situation and bring the matter to a satisfactory conclusion. Today, here in this Hampshire country house, he would complete the business which had already kept him in England too long.

Three more men entered the room—Colonel Itzhak Yaacobi, who had traveled from Israel at one hour's notice, an ex-British major representing the British Foreign Office and a good looking man with untidy fair hair carrying his arm in a sling. Reylord greeted each of them, discovering the third man was Steven Marsh of whom he had recently heard a great deal. John Reylord found no difficulty in believing Marsh would be a tough character. He was not entirely sure why he had been asked to attend.

As though instinctively knowing everyone was here, the few quiet pockets of conversation died as people automatically moved to their chairs. Reylord remained standing at the end of the table waiting for the doors to be discreetly closed from outside. He successfully combated the urge to light another cigarette. Clearing his throat he began his carefully prepared opening address.

Much of what Reylord had to say was of interest to Marsh who had been instructed to attend the meeting rather against his will. He listened, trying unsuccessfully to forget what had happened two days ago in Anacortes. So bloody easy, he thought, you sit round a table and talk. Then, if you're lucky, some important bastard makes a decision which sends some man or woman halfway across the world to get their heads blown off. He sat ignoring the biting ache in his side where they had sewn him up.

"Gentlemen," Reylord said with a sweeping glance

round his audience. "We are here to clear the air once and for all. When we have done so we will endeavor to decide upon the most suitable attitude for NATO to adopt in such difficult circumstances. I regret the necessity to direct my next remarks to Colonel Yaacobi who, as the sole representative of Israel, can only wonder at the events which have followed NATO's abortive attempts to recover the Kfir missile data."

Yaacobi stared coldly at the chairman knowing full well that Reylord could not possibly disclose the truth. He watched the American lose his own battle and reach for a cigarette.

"Firstly," Reylord continued, "both the British and American governments have formally expressed their regret at having failed to bring this unfortunate matter to a satisfactory conclusion." Conscious of the fact that he was lapsing into official jargon, he smiled. "I think it is safe to reveal the truth within the walls of this room—you will forgive me, therefore, if I tread heavily on some toes." The smile vanished and Reylord's expression hardened. "NATO, gentlemen, has failed utterly to work in the common interests of the West and has failed Israel in more ways than one.

"The British, for their own interests, have deliberately tried to mislead the United States and the United States has been guilty not only of negligence in its internal security but has also attempted to assist Israel by itself instead of working within NATO. Incredibly, a complete set of false drawings was prepared in order to confuse the Americans whilst the CIA seems to have made a point of announcing every one of their moves to the organization originally responsible for stealing the data from Israel's missile plant. This whole sorry affair is an extraordinary story of violence and incompetence culminating in disaster for every western nation. And the information, gentlemen, the Kfir missile design data, is now back in the hands of those Anglo-American companies who are so vitally interested in breaking the Arab trade boycott."

Yaacobi stood up. "If we are here to clear the air," he said pointedly, "Israel is entitled to request a full explanation. If a reoccurrence of such bungling is to be prevented it would undoubtedly be useful to explore the reasons behind the strange competitiveness existing between Britain and the U.S."

Reylord stared angrily at him. "I think the reasons are outside the scope or references of this meeting, Colonel. I also think you know very well that no one here can answer your question."

The Colonel remained standing, his face grim. "In that case I have been asked to answer the question for you. Israel will not be taken for a fool and we will not forget this. The Jews have long memories, gentlemen. I will answer my own question in order to clear the air as our chairman suggests, and I will answer it in one word. Oil, gentlemen, oil. And before I sit down may I say that Israel would not treat her friends and allies as you have treated Israel. We understand what has motivated the West and we despise the organizations and the men who have pretended to help us. That is all." Yaacobi sat down watching the eyes of the other men. Only Steven Marsh appeared unmoved by his statement.

Reylord's face was the face of a man striving for control. He answered Yaacobi very quietly. "You have the assurance of NATO that a repeat of this will not occur. My terms of reference are precise, Colonel, and you will have to be content with the official apologies your government has already received. Now it is—"

Still seated Yaacobi interrupted him. "What did the United States stand to gain in supplying Israel with faked drawings? And would Israel have received an apology if we had not eventually drawn the matter to your attention? We also wonder how any handover of the genuine drawings could have been reconciled with the presentation of the false ones we did receive. And what, precisely, did the British have in mind?"

The American ambassador rose to his feet together with the representative from the British Foreign Office.

Knowing it was absolutely essential to prevent the confrontation which was about to erupt, Reylord raised his voice. "Gentlemen," he said with force. "Please sit down. Colonel Yaacobi is in fact fully aware of the answers to his own questions as he has already told us. As a chairman of this meeting I cannot permit you to interrupt proceedings in this way. There have been many mistakes and those responsible for them will be brought to account. Meanwhile I must insist that this particular avenue of questioning is abandoned. You have all been briefed on the purpose of this gathering and I remind you all of your own terms of reference. I intend to continue with my address and ask you to remain silent until I have finished. When I have concluded we will discuss the future, gentlemen—not the past."

There was the click of cigarette lighters and a number of low murmurs but Reylord had regained control. He knew it would be necessary to skip much of what he had intended to say if further trouble was to be avoided and John Reylord was more than anxious to avoid trouble.

He paused until he was sure of attention before speaking again.

"Although there has been severe mismanagement in this affair, I am able to reveal more encouraging information which is not known to the majority of you and which is of great significance to all of us. I am pleased to say we now know—or think we know—the names of the companies involved in the conspiracy. Two days ago the president of the Federation of Anglo-American Companies received a telephone call from a certain gentleman in San Francisco. British Intelligence have been monitoring such calls for some time and on this occasion the message which Mr. Dryden received was of a sufficiently suspicious nature for them to immediately undertake a more extensive investigation."

Certain now that he had the undivided attention of every man in the room, Reylord lit another cigarette enjoying his moment of power.

"Mr. Dryden, gentlemen, left for Beirut in haste. As far as we know he is there at this very minute where he is shortly to be joined by a Mr. Edward Cabinda who is believed to be in possession of the Kfir missile drawings. The British and American security agencies have established this fairly certainly and, after what has happened, I imagine we should all be grateful for the information.

"Mr. Dryden traveled first to Paris where his colleagues still believe him to be—Mr. Cabinda flew directly to Lebanon from the United States. Unfortunately his departure was made some hours before the CIA were informed of what had taken place and they decided to do nothing but arrange for his continued surveillance.

"Since this information has been received, all major air terminals in the United States and here in Great Britain have been under intensive scrutiny and as a result we have been able to monitor the travel arrangements of certain men representing a number of large Anglo-American companies. By now I'm sure you will have realized what has been established. Twelve senior executives—I repeat twelve—have in the last twenty-four hours left their respective countries to travel to Lebanon. Without exception their final destination has been Beirut and without exception they have all chosen to make their way there by what can only be described as indirect routes. The conclusions are, I think, quite clear and we can now be sure that an important meeting is about to be convened with the Arabs to negotiate a selective removal of their trade bloc."

Reylord paused again before glancing round the table to determine the effect of his revelation. "We have the names of the men and companies concerned. The president of the FAAC has shown himself to be a renegade and a traitor and probably the instigator of this whole unsavory affair. Cabinda, however, is believed to be a free-lance operator hired to deliver the drawings at the appropriate time and place—I also understand he is a violent and dangerous man."

Steven Marsh thought that Cabinda must have moved like greased lightning to get out of the States in time. Less than an hour had elapsed between the time the Anacortes police had dragged him bleeding from the gutter and the time that the CIA had arrived at his hospital bed with their endless questions. With Sharmila gone—disappearing without trace—he had told Dahl everything as soon as he had arrived from San Francisco—yet still Cabinda had slipped through the CIA's fingers.

Until now Marsh had clung to the belief that Sharmila had somehow managed to return alone to Israel with the drawings. What he had just heard had shattered his last vestiges of hope. A tremendous need for revenge was making it impossible for him to listen to what Reylord was saying and he was seeing the room through a dull haze.

Gripping the arms of his chair Marsh deliberately made himself sweat with self-induced pain from his bullet wound. Why the hell couldn't they have told him before? Why wait until now in a room full of men who could never understand what had happened between an Israeli girl and a British agent. He wanted to say her name—wanted to shout that they had killed her. Cabinda was on his way to Beirut and that meant he had the drawings—Sharmila was dead, for she would have found him long ago if she was still alive. Anger, bitterness and the blinding need to avenge her—he fought it knowing he could do nothing but live with her memory and perhaps one day find this Cabinda and make him pay for what he had done—kill him as he had killed Sharmila.

Reylord was winding down. He closed his file before announcing a brief break for coffee.

At once men quietly left the table and formed small groups to discuss what they had learned.

Warren Dahl sought out Marsh who also had remained seated. The American sat down wearily beside him. "I guess we won't find the girl now," he said, unaware of his unfortunate choice of opening.

Marsh turned. "You don't understand, Dahl," he said. "Just leave it alone, will you."

"I have a couple of questions," Dahl said, "and I won't have the chance to ask you again. Tell me about the Firebird and those goddam drawings you planted. You never got around to it before you left the States."

Marsh told him, feeling almost sorry for the CIA man. When he had finished Dahl looked even more depressed. Both men drank their coffee in silence, each busy with his own thoughts.

"If you'd found your own leak in San Francisco," Marsh said, "you could've got on to Cabinda. He must've had a private line into your department right up to the time when you spotted us leaving Seattle. He even got an aircraft on our tail when we flew out of Reno—Cabinda was better organized than you and he didn't have a security problem either. You'd better start looking."

Dahl shook his head. "We cleaned out his organization yesterday. Five of them and one in my San Francisco office. We're holding them for the murder of Max Navon, but they're already filling in the story for us. Sure Cabinda had a good organization once—now it doesn't exist."

"Now he doesn't need it," Marsh answered. "The bastard was ahead of you all the way—maybe if we'd really worked together you'd still have a job, Israel would have got the drawings back and Sharmila would still be alive."

Dahl sensed something. "She was a MOSSAD agent, you know what that means as well as I do. I wouldn't waste too much time on any regrets in that direction, Marsh."

"And I've said I don't want to talk about it," Marsh replied. "Next time I'm in San Francisco I'll buy you a drink, but until then you still work for the lousy CIA and I don't. I'll see you later, Dahl."

The American rose from his chair and rejoined the U.S. ambassador. Simultaneously Reylord called the meeting to order. He wasted no time in preliminaries.

"Now I have outlined the progress we have made it is necessary for us to determine the most expedient way of bringing these companies to heel. The following proposal is for your consideration—"

Colonel Yaacobi was on his feet again. "I apologize for a further interruption but I cannot allow you to continue. I must ask you to be kind enough to allow me to make a statement."

"May I have your assurance that you will avoid all comments of a deliberately contentious nature?" Reylord wished the Colonel had remained in Jerusalem.

"Of course," Yaacobi nodded. "I will not take much of the meeting's time. Whilst it is commendable that the West will take immediate steps to put their house in order you must appreciate that Israel has no intention of allowing the matter to rest in Lebanon. As I speak to you now, preparations are being made to launch an attack on the hotel in Beirut where the meeting is scheduled to take place. I am astonished that Israel has not been offered assistance in this respect although in the circumstances it is unnecessary and would not be accepted. However, on behalf of my government, I wish to formally request your political cooperation and say that in particular Israel expects the

American and British news media to support the action
—in moderation naturally."

This time Reylord was visibly annoyed. "The West
cannot and will not give you any such assurance. Should
Israel be successful in preventing the Arabs from taking
the drawings away with them the West will be relieved
but we certainly cannot officially condone a terrorist
attack on a Lebanese hotel."

Yaacobi smiled slightly. "In view of your past performance your reluctance is not entirely unexpected.
However, may I remind you of the vicious and unpro-
voked Palestinian fedayeen raid three days ago in the
streets of Tel Aviv in which fourteen innocent people
were shot dead. You are aware of Israel's attitude to
such attacks by the Arabs. We will retaliate in our
normal way and on this occasion, to use one of your
expressions, we intend to kill two birds with one stone.
The West can surely express their understanding of the
Israeli code for a change thus removing any possible
suggestion of their own involvement which might be
made."

No one had missed the Colonel's point. A few worried faces showed round the table whilst men tried to
assess the seriousness of Yaacobi's carefully worded
threat. If Israel chose to publicize her own suitably
edited reason for the raid and hint that it had been
carried out with the active assistance of Britain and
America, untold harm could be done to already delicate
relations with the Arabs. The oil crisis would hardly
be eased by such publicity.

To protect his own position, Reylord felt it vital to
answer the Colonel on behalf of all members of the
meeting. "Now if you will forgive a rather sudden
change of attitude, I now believe it is in the best interests of everyone to make sure that the news media
avoid all unfavorable comment on Israel's retaliatory
raid, Colonel Yaacobi. It is perhaps the least the West
can do."

Yaacobi had not finished. The confident smile remained on his face.

"Israel requests one favor," he said. "The provision of an observer to positively identify Cabinda. It is important for us to be sure."

Marsh slowly stood up. "You've got one, Colonel," he said, "and if you'll have me I'd like you to make it clear that you aren't prepared to consider anyone else —I've got a few cards, too. I'd like to go anyway."

"Please sit down, Mr. Marsh," Reylord said stonily. "You are out of order. The matter will not be discussed here."

Yaacobi closed the file in front of him. "Israel insists on the presence of Mr. Marsh. He will accompany me. And I have nothing more to say."

His face suffused with blood, John Reylord was furious. "I will not allow this meeting to degenerate into a discussion on a terrorist raid and you are certainly in no position to volunteer to act as an observer, Marsh. Should NATO decide to assist Israel by supplying one, the matter will have to be discussed at a much higher level."

The ex-British major from the Foreign Office felt it necessary to exert his authority. He said, "Quite so," naïvely believing his words would settle the matter.

Marsh looked first at Reylord then at the ex-major. "Balls," he said pleasantly. "There isn't time and I don't think you understand what Colonel Yaacobi has told you. Israel is going to fix up this whole bloody mess for you and unless the West makes the right noises afterwards she's going to make damn sure the British and Americans get the blame. So you just sit here and worry about your oil prices and let Israel get on with it. I'm going because I'm the best choice you've got and because Colonel Yaacobi has said he can use me." He glanced at Yaacobi. "How about leaving these gentlemen to make their important decisions without us —we might need to hurry from what I've heard."

Yaacobi was unable to keep a straight face. "With your permission, John," he said to Reylord. "Mr. Marsh and I would be grateful if you could continue any discussions with us another time. Mr. Marsh is quite correct—we have urgent business elsewhere."

John Reylord recovered his composure with some difficulty. "I will be in touch with your embassy," he said. "Meanwhile if you must leave at such an inopportune moment then we will have to excuse you. Your presence here today has hardly been beneficial—perhaps matters will proceed more smoothly without you."

Gathering his papers from the table Yaacobi nodded a cool good-bye to the members of the meeting. Marsh joined him at the door. Reylord made no further remarks waiting silently with his back to them.

As Marsh left the room he saw Dahl wink at him.

CHAPTER FIFTEEN

Steven Marsh had learned a great deal in a very short time. During the long flight from London, Yaacobi had spoken almost without stopping, providing Marsh with what he considered to be rather more information than was strictly necessary. His first favorable impression of Yaacobi had quickly been confirmed and by the time they landed in Tel Aviv a warm friendship had formed between the two men.

The Colonel had avoided discussing the reason behind Marsh's request to participate in the raid, giving the impression either that he somehow or other understood the Englishman's need for revenge or that the reason was unimportant to him. Because of this apparent disinterest, Marsh had become conscious of the need to offer what he could in the way of an explanation and several times referred to events he had shared with Sharmila during the few days they had spent together. On each occasion Yaacobi had listened with interest but displayed no desire to probe more deeply. In the end, Marsh had given up, deciding that if the Colonel was prepared to accept him on face value he could do no less than stop looking for hidden reasons behind the Israeli's willingness to allow him along for the ride.

The Institute—as Yaacobi called MOSSAD—was far larger and more organized than Marsh had been led to believe. Although he already had a good working knowledge of Israeli Intelligence, he had been surprised to discover how much it had grown since its creation in 1972. Without appearing to brag, Yaacobi had listed some of its more recent successes, describing numerous missions in which the Institute had sought out and killed Palestinians known to be connected with recurring fedayeen attacks on Israeli townships near the border. Marsh had been genuinely impressed.

Once in Tel Aviv, Yaacobi had spared time only to phone his wife in Jerusalem before beginning final preparations for the Beirut attack. Using a tiny office in one of the military establishments on the northern outskirts of town he had organized matters so rapidly that Marsh soon realized Colonel Yaacobi was no ordinary Colonel. By lunchtime today everything was ready for stage two of the operation.

Stage one was already complete. Six spotters—five men and a young woman—had left an airfield in northern Israel at 8:30 the night before. Keeping their faces covered so that not even members of their chopper crew would be able to identify them they had stowed their guns and equipment on board an Israeli air force Bell 205 helicopter and headed north for Beirut. A second helicopter had accompanied them acting as a gunship.

Flying a carefully chosen route along the border between Lebanon and Syria so that radar networks in either country would assume the two helicopters were on routine missions from the other side, the spotters were landed one hour later in an area not far from Beirut itself. The protecting gunship had not been required, its presence overhead being reassuring but unnecessary whilst the spotters were met by waiting Israeli agents.

As the spotters were driven to a safe house in the Beirut suburbs both helicopters returned undetected to report an uneventful and successful delivery. Yaacobi had received the information calmly, telling Marsh that this was the fourth time the same method had been used to land agents deep inside Lebanese territory.

Throughout the day in the sweltering heat of Yaacobi's temporary office, both men had sustained themselves on endless cups of black coffee waiting for the spotters to confirm the presence of Dryden and the others in the Beirut hotel.

At eleven in the morning the third coded radio message was eventually received. By midday it had become essential to complete Yaacobi's plan with all speed.

Replacing his telephone Yaacobi used his handkerchief to wipe beads of perspiration from his brow. "It's going to have to be tonight," he said. "We are already nearly too late. If I had not gone to London it would have been finished by now."

Marsh smiled wearily at him. "And then you wouldn't have had anyone to identify Cabinda."

"We would have found him, Steven. From what you have told me of him he might well have evaded our people but later we would have found him."

"What did they say on the phone?" Marsh asked.

"Your Mr. Dryden is at the hotel. Eight American executives and four British executives are also there. This morning three prominent Arab leaders arrived to take up advanced reservations in their own names. The entire third floor of the building is being used for an international trade convention. Is that enough?"

"Cabinda?" Marsh inquired.

Yaacobi shook his head. "No one of that name but he'll be there."

"And what's the hurry all of a sudden?"

The Colonel pushed a button on the telephone. "One of our men checked out the air terminal. Seven of the executives leave Beirut tomorrow morning."

"That gives us tonight," Marsh said. "That's okay."

"We have to get there and get back," Yaacobi reminded him. "And getting back might prove just a little difficult."

A sergeant entered the room.

Yaacobi unfolded a map on his desk. "I want two navy missile boats to leave the Haifa base inside the hour. They will each carry three Zodiac rubber dinghies. They will proceed up the coast as if on a routine mission. At a predetermined time tonight the dinghies will be waiting here." He placed a finger on the map. "The usual radio frequency will be used—do you have any questions?"

"I will need the exact time an hour in advance of the rendezvous, sir; the navy will have to wait well off shore."

"You'll have it before that," Yaacobi said. "And I want one helicopter for the dropping zone we used last night—I'll give you the time I require it later this afternoon."

"No gunship this time?" Marsh asked.

"If they pick up a single chopper on their radar they might let it go—but two, two nights running is more than suspicious." Yaacobi refolded the map. "I'd rather not risk a helicopter at all but you and I must be there and it's the only way. I have grown cautious in my old age, Steven."

Caution, Marsh thought, was not a characteristic he had associated with Yaacobi. In the late nineteen-seventies Colonel Yaacobi was closer to a dashing man of action than anyone he had come across for a very long time. With men like him controlling Israel's underground operations she could hardly fail to survive. Marsh hoped Israel's destiny would remain in the hands of such men.

"We could go in by boat," Marsh said.

Yaacobi shook his head. "Too messy and not quick enough. One hour in a Bell 205 and we will be close enough to Beirut to be at the hotel sixty minutes after we have been dropped."

The sergeant made ready to leave. "You will require frogmen to secure the beach, sir."

"Sub-machine-guns and grenades—emergency use only," Yaacobi replied. "That will be all, Sergeant—thank you."

Now all final arrangements for stage two had been completed Marsh could feel the excitement beginning to make his spine tingle. "I want a gun," he said quietly. "You can't really afford to have me without one, can you?"

Yaacobi smiled. "There was no need to ask—we are a very practical people. Another weapon in experienced hands could make the difference between success and failure. I would not have allowed you to come with us if I believed you could do nothing more than identify the American Cabinda. When it is over you can tell me why it is your eyes are so angry and why you are so anxious to help Israel after working against her on your last assignment."

Marsh was again tempted to say something to remove any doubts Yaacobi might have about him but was prevented from doing so by the arrival of the army doctor Yaacobi had requested earlier.

The Colonel stated his position very clearly. "Two men who are already very fatigued will be sent out on a vital mission this evening. It is essential for them to remain fully alert until early tomorrow morning."

"Pills," the doctor stated bluntly. "And an injection before you leave." He inspected Marsh. "You are going with Colonel Yaacobi?"

"That's right," Marsh said. "Why?"

The doctor shook his head sadly. "Show me your arm."

Yaacobi interrupted. "A gunshot wound doctor, it will not deter Mr. Marsh from accompanying me."

"I can strap it to your side," the doctor offered.

Marsh shook his head. "I might just need it—if I do you can sew me up again when I get back."

The doctor turned on his heel and left the room.

"We must leave soon for the airfield, Steven," Yaacobi said. "We can talk on the way." He reached into his shirt pocket and produced a crumpled blue envelope. For a second Marsh believed he was going to pass it to him but Yaacobi changed his mind and withdrew his hand.

"Lunch," the Colonel said suddenly. "And then we will get ready."

After a light meal at the military base, both men were outfitted by a special MOSSAD department consisting of four efficient young women who seemed to have an inexhaustible supply of civilian clothing at their disposal. For fifteen minutes Marsh was critically examined in a variety of shirts and trousers, each change causing him to wince with the pain from his wound.

Totally unsympathetic and ruthlessly efficient he was not permitted to go until they were satisfied. For most of the time Yaacobi watched him struggle into shirt after shirt with evident amusement. When it was over Marsh was presented with a .22 caliber Beretta pistol.

"What the hell's the use of this?" he said to Yaacobi.

The Colonel showed him his own weapon. It was identical. "You will have to believe that we have much experience in raids of this kind," he said. "We will be working in a very confined space and the Beretta is the most accurate hand gun in the world. What it lacks in stopping power is more than compensated for by its accuracy. In the hands of trained men it is deadly and we use only trained men. Such a small weapon is also extremely easy to conceal—that is very important."

In no position to argue, Marsh slid his gun into the pocket of his trousers finding his left hand clumsy in an experimental draw. He took a handful of ammunition and shrugged his shoulders.

"Try carrying it inside your sling," Yaacobi suggested.

"I'll mess around with it later," Marsh said. "Are we finished here?"

"We are. We must now transfer to the airfield at Acre. First we will go for our jab as you call it in English then we will board a commercial aircraft which is waiting for us here in Tel Aviv. It will be good to be moving again."

It was gone four o'clock in the afternoon before they left Tel Aviv terminal for the short flight northwards. Feeling brighter than he had done for some days under the influence of the injection, Marsh enjoyed the journey along the Mediterranean coast, spending his time gazing from the window at an almost unbroken shore line curving its way towards Lebanon.

From the air the sea was a piercing cobalt blue and he was able to obtain an impression of Israel not possible from the ground. A narrow strip of arid land with Egypt to the south, Jordan to the east and Lebanon and Syria at the northern tip. Home of the Jewish nation who for so long had been fighting for its own place in the Middle East. And tonight, in Beirut, Israel would strike yet another blow in her unique crusade—Marsh wondered how long she could endure the war of nerves which had been waged against her for so many years.

He turned to Yaacobi sitting beside him. "You really believe in this eye for an eye business, don't you?" he asked.

Yaacobi nodded. "Month after month, year after year the terrorists cross our borders to maim and kill our people. One day they will learn that we will never stop our policy of retaliation. The West does not or cannot understand, but how else will we convince our enemies that their attacks will do nothing but harden Israel's heart against them?"

"Sometimes countering violence with violence makes no sense," Marsh answered. "But I'm not a Jew so maybe I don't understand either."

The Colonel smiled. "We know more about you than you believe. Your father died in Dachau, Steven Marsh—he was half Jewish and he died because of it. You are here with me now because of that and because of something else. Sometimes every man needs to avenge a wrong and an eye for an eye or a tooth for a tooth is a philosophy which lives in every one of us. Do not judge a nation when you yourself yield to the very same need."

Marsh remembered the file Sharmila had mentioned to him. "My reasons are my own Colonel but I wouldn't want you to really think I don't understand how an Israeli thinks. I do, very well." He meant what he said and he wished he could stop thinking of Sharmila.

All too soon the nose of the plane dropped and the brief flight was over. They were met by three airforce officers, men who would fly the helicopter into Lebanon.

For the few remaining hours they waited on a remote airstrip for the sun to sink below the horizon counting the minutes as the take-off time drew nearer.

Although not expected, no further radio messages had been received from the spotting team who, Yaacobi hoped, had been busily at work outside and inside the Liban hotel in the Rue Riad el-Solh for most of the afternoon.

The temperature was still twenty-five degrees when it was finally dark enough to begin the one-hour flight to the dropping zone.

Damp from perspiration and with the effect of the injection gone long ago, Marsh climbed into the Bell helicopter thankful that their wait was over. Despite fatigue and the pain from his wound he was experiencing the feeling of elation which always precedes a mission of this kind.

"How's the arm?" Yaacobi shouted over the roar of the engine.

Marsh grimaced and made a rude sign knowing the Colonel's question was deliberately insincere. "If I'd been shot with one of your toy Berettas," he yelled, "I probably wouldn't even have known about it."

Also aware of the artificial sensation of being invulnerable and unbeatable, Yaacobi grinned at the Englishman wondering as he did so if both of them would return safely. As the helicopter gained altitude and headed for the border separating Syria from Lebanon, the Colonel thought about his wife at home in Jerusalem. On this occasion he managed to think of her for nearly fifty-five minutes.

Fifty-seven minutes from the time the helicopter had left Israel it landed softly on Lebanese soil to discharge its two passengers. No sudden gunfire flashed from the surrounding darkness and no armored vehicles rushed to encircle the helicopter as Marsh and Yaacobi ran crouching from the cockpit hatchway.

The Colonel waited for the Bell to chop its way noisily upwards through the night air before using his flashlight to signal their arrival. If things had gone wrong this would be the time for surprises.

But nothing had gone wrong. There was an answering flash, the sound of a car starting and the rendezvous had been completed without any of the hitches which so easily could lead to disaster.

Minutes later the commander of the raid was on the road to Beirut.

In the back seat of the car Steven Marsh was practicing holding his Beretta in his right hand.

CHAPTER SIXTEEN

Beirut, half a million people, the busy capital of Lebanon and a city where for the first time in his life Marsh was to play the role of executioner. He lit a cigarette and leaned back against the railings outside the Liban hotel only half-listening to the girl beside him.

Not as pretty as Sharmila, he thought, but roughly the same age and with the same innocent look. Maybe MOSSAD recruited them deliberately.

"We used rifles last time," she said in the perfect English Marsh had learned to expect. "Fitted with starlight telescopic sights—do you know the ones?"

Marsh nodded. "But you didn't have to deal with a whole hotel floor, did you?"

"No, just one Palestinian. We shot him through his bedroom window. We were on a roof on the opposite side of the road. He'd organized a raid on Jaffa a month before and deserved to die. The PLO murdered three Israeli children when they attacked."

Marsh didn't want to hear about it. As he'd told Yaacobi, he was here for his own reasons and had no wish to become deeply involved in the Middle East terrorist war. Once this was over he'd get the hell out of it, then try to decide what to do with what remained of his life—if anything remained.

He glanced at his watch. "Ten minutes," he said to the girl. "Let me see the photographs again."

She handed him an envelope which he placed in his shirt pocket withdrawing the polaroid shots one at a time and using the street light to inspect them.

There were four pictures of Dryden, all of them taken outside the hotel from a range of at least a hundred yards. Without exception they were of poor quality despite good lighting and the best concealed lens which could be fitted to the cameras the spotters had used. None of the photos showed any real detail of Dryden's face and Marsh was not confident of identifying him in a hurry if the need arose.

Some of the executives had been photographed with greater success but there was a depressing sameness about the men and, although Marsh knew he should make an effort to remember each and every one of them, his mood was such that he found himself unable to concentrate properly. There was no picture of the man known as Edward Cabinda.

The lights along the Rue Riad el-Solh twinkled brightly and the evening traffic was as frantic and noisy as any other city that Marsh could remember. There was a smell of the Middle East combined with a bustle of people which seemed characteristically Lebanese, but still Marsh could not completely overcome the feeling of being somewhere else, let alone combat the atmosphere of unreality which surrounded the whole mission. The suddenness of his arrival in Beirut, the awareness of being completely detached from the hate between Israel and the PLO and the most recent dose of stimulant pills was making him view everything as though he was not part of it. It was still extremely warm.

He returned the photographs to the girl. "And I suppose you've been asked to look after me?" he asked.

She smiled. "I know you don't want me to."

He changed the subject. "Did you know Sharmila Talmai?"

"No, why?"

"Nothing. She was a friend of mine. She worked for the Institute too."

She moved closer to him. "Look over there by the hotel entrance."

Four soldiers had emerged from the front door to stand guard. Each of them carried an automatic rifle.

Marsh put an arm round her waist. "Maybe we should move."

"There isn't time, we've got to be inside in less than a minute."

A Citroën drew up outside the hotel. Yaacobi and two other men got out and walked laughing up to the front door ignoring the presence of the guards. One of the Israelis carried a suitcase.

Marsh forced himself to wait until they had disappeared into the foyer before he led the girl across the road towards the same entrance. Fifteen yards away from the guards he gently guided her to a tree beside one of the floodlit fountains. In full view of the four men they embraced and kissed each other.

"Now we go in," Marsh whispered. "Are you frightened?"

"Yes, are you?"

No, Marsh thought suddenly, I'm not and I damned well should be. "Sure," he said. "Come on." He wished there was more than revenge to drive him on. Pointless revenge was not enough and the feeling of detachment was even stronger.

Hand in hand, their eyes on each other, they left the tree and walked to the swing doors. Incredibly she managed to giggle as they climbed the steps. The guards paid no attention to them.

A half dozen people were milling about in the foyer and one of the Israeli spotters stepped casually from the elevator as they stood watching. He disappeared in the direction of the ground floor dining-room.

To their left was the wide carpeted stairway they had been told to use. They had forty-five seconds in which to reach the third floor. Of Yaacobi and the other two Israelis there was no sign.

Already Marsh was doubting the possibility of success. Seven men and a girl might just manage to retrieve the drawings and kill as many of the occupants on the floor as Yaacobi wanted to, but there was no certain way for eight people to return through the foyer and get out of Lebanon alive. Not even eight people to carry out the raid he realized. One spotter had been made responsible for the car, another for deactivating the elevator and a third would secure the foyer ready for their escape. Only five of them against Dryden, Cabinda and God knows how many security guards the Arab leaders had brought with them. He wondered if Cabinda was really here.

At the second floor the girl stopped to pass him an envelope. It was the same one he'd seen in Yaacobi's hand shortly before they had left Tel Aviv.

"Colonel Yaacobi asked me to make sure you read this," she said. "I've left it a bit late I'm afraid."

An American aerogram postmarked Seattle. It was addressed to the Minister of Foreign Affairs in Israel.

Marsh unfolded it and read the contents hardly able to believe what he was seeing. The effect of the letter on the Englishman had been predicted exactly by the Israeli Colonel who had purposely delayed showing it to him in order to extract every scrap of benefit that it could provide.

In comparison with the sudden and dramatic change in Steven Marsh which the letter produced, the lift from stimulants he had received in the last eight hours was so trivial that Yaacobi would have been deeply gratified.

Beside Marsh, the Israeli girl had sufficient time to see his face change before he began climbing the last flight of stairs to the third floor.

More alive and more dangerous than he had been for many an assignment, Marsh drew his Beretta as

ne reached the landing. Simultaneously a wood paneled door opened directly in front of him. Two armed
Lebanese soldiers stepped out.

Letting his pistol drop, Marsh's hand flew out to
seize the throat of the second man. Reacting with commendable speed, the first soldier was on the point of
crying out and leveling his gun when the Englishman's
knee caught him brutally in the groin. Vomiting and
clutching himself between the legs he fell to his knees
making a bubbling, moaning noise.

For a second Marsh released his grip on the throat
of the other man. Fighting for precious oxygen he began to drop, then his body was driven sideways as
Marsh chopped down savagely on his neck with the
edge of his hand.

Before Marsh could step back to complete his work
the Israeli girl was busy with her knife. He looked
away.

"We're late now," she said, retrieving his gun with
a bloody hand.

Wordlessly Marsh helped her drag the bodies inside
the door. He inspected his watch finding they were
twenty seconds behind schedule.

A poorly lit corridor stretched ahead of them to the
closed glass doors of a conference room at the far end.
Beside him on the wall a plastic noticeboard announced
the meeting of the trade delegation in both Arabic and
English lettering.

Earlier today in that room the final deal would have
been made with the Arabs and now, Marsh thought, the
unsuspecting members would be relaxing somewhere
in one or more of the twenty rooms which they were
going to have to search. In the next two hundred and
twenty seconds four MOSSAD agents and one Englishman had to destroy the network Dryden had built,
recover the drawings and carry out one more critical
job.

For Marsh, the mission had taken on such a dif-

ferent complexion that even the prospect of facing
Cabinda on level terms was was of little or no consequence to him. The cruel, unnecessary retribution
which the Israelis were about to mete out was their
business, and now Marsh knew he was not a part of it
at all. Revenge no longer mattered—only one single,
vital thing was important.

At the end of the corridor Yaacobi and two spotters
appeared from the swing doors of the conference room.
It was time.

He saw Yaacobi start taking wads of plastic explosives from the suitcase and mold them on to some
of the bedroom doors lining either side of the pas-
sageway. When he had finished, nearly fifty pounds of
the stuff would be in place. Another man was following
the Colonel sticking timers and detonators into the soft
plasticine lumps. Shortly before Yaacobi reached him
Marsh collected the carbines left by the two dead
guards passing one to the grim-faced Israeli. Yaacobi
held up ten fingers, took the carbine with a nod and
ran lightly back to the other end of the corridor. His
accomplice returned more slowly, setting each timer
as he went.

"Outside, away from the door," Marsh whispered to
the girl. "Quickly."

Stepping over the bodies they opened the door into
the faces of four well-dressed English businessmen.

Heart beating, carbine in hand, Marsh smiled politely holding the door for them as they passed by. As-
tonishingly, they ignored him completely, glancing only
briefly at the girl.

No sooner had they entered the corridor than the
explosive went off. In such a restricted space the tremendous blast was channeled outwards along the narrow confines of the passage.

Bleeding from their mouths, two of the businessmen
staggered backwards through the broken door which
had swung outwards with such force that what was

left of it narrowly missed the girl sheltering with her back to the wall. Marsh let them go but immediately readied the carbine. The raid had begun in earnest.

Acrid smoke was billowing past him hiding the girl as she slipped away to begin her work. Marsh never saw her again.

There was a fusillade of shots accompanied by the sound of splintering wood. He counted, willing himself to stay where he was until he was completely ready to move.

Cradling the carbine against his left hip he eased himself round the doorframe conscious now of a growing fear which at last had come to make his hands tremble and his knees feel weak.

Strangely, some of the lights had not been broken by the fearful blast but smoke still hung in the air making it difficult to see what was happening. The corridor appeared deserted apart from the bodies of the two other executives lying on the floor. One of them was moving slightly.

Gritting his teeth he forced himself to approach the first closed door, one that had not been blown off its hinges. It took two shots from the carbine then he burst in ready to fight for his life. The room was unoccupied.

He turned in time to see an Arab guard raise his gun. Marsh shot him in the stomach, jumped over him as he fell and headed for the door.

Before he reached the corridor the sound of almost continuous small arms fire echoed deafeningly from the end under Yaacobi's control.

Now there were men everywhere, desperate men striving to identify each other in the smoke and struggling for their very lives in the semi-darkness.

Despair seized him. Twenty rooms, maybe more than twenty men. Yaacobi was utterly mad to have ever believed it could be done. And there wasn't time.

Still holding the carbine in his left hand he slid his right arm from the sling and in one awful jerk freed it from the restriction of his stitches. For a second the pain was blinding then he had the Beretta in his right hand and Steven Marsh made up his mind. Now or bloody never. All or nothing—now.

The next room—two Americans crouching in terror behind the bed—leave them. Four guards in the passage, one already wounded the others scared out of their wits. He shot one with the Beretta and sprang backwards into another room nearly tripping over. No one followed and the room was empty.

Sub-machine-gun fire. God, they'd never get out. The sound of a man screaming and then for two long, terrible seconds complete silence.

Three rooms and two dead men later he felt a bullet smack into the muscle on his right thigh. A small caliber bullet or his leg would have become instantly useless. Blood from his old wound ran down his side to mix with the blood oozing from the fresh puncture.

More smoke and barely enough light to pick out stumbling men appearing before him like figures in a nightmare.

The next door was open but there was no evidence of shattered wood on the frame beside the handle. A trap—but there was no time left.

Throwing what remained of any caution he might once have had to the winds or to the Gods who had kept him alive this far, he leapt through the opening. Simultaneously there was the phut from a gun Marsh recognized. Unscathed, in a low crouch, he saw Cabinda smile as he aimed again.

Marsh tried vainly to roll out of the way whilst he fought to make his wounded arm raise his own gun quickly enough. But he had forgotten what Yaacobi had said about the .22 Beretta.

Knowing it was all over Marsh made one last wild effort and squeezed the trigger. A small hole—a very neat red hole—appeared in the center of Cabinda's forehead.

The lifeless body of the man who had tried so hard to kill Steven Marsh toppled slowly forward to form an untidy heap on the carpet.

And in one corner of the room, her hands shackled to the towel rail, a young Israeli girl wept with relief.

He used the carbine on the short steel chain bruising her wrists terribly but freeing her with the fourth shot. No one entered the room to fire a fatal bullet in his back whilst he worked, yet neither he nor the girl uttered a single word. There would be time to talk later if they survived.

Just as they were ready to leave Marsh heard Jaacobi's whistle.

Giving her the Beretta he ran to the door almost colliding with one of the spotters, both men almost on the point of firing at each other. The spotter was badly wounded in the face.

"Use the stairs," he muttered and staggered away.

"Let's go," Marsh breathed, "and please God get us both out of here alive."

Three flights of stairs later they entered the foyer to find Yaacobi and two other MOSSAD agents waiting for them. Bodies of Palestinian guards littered the floor.

"Back door," Yaacobi instructed curtly.

Colonel Yaacobi, one spotter, Steven Marsh and Sharmila Talmai made the Citroën. Counting the driver, five people left the Liban hotel alive. Less than six minutes earlier this evening eight Israelis had arrived to carry out a double mission of retaliation and recovery. Of these only four had survived, the fifth passenger in the car being the girl who had been rescued in the first successful undertaking of this kind that the Institute had ever attempted.

Clinging to Marsh, Sharmila felt blood warm and sticky on her hands but she knew it was still too early to speak.

Using all of the road, the driver held the car in second gear bursting his way through the traffic with a

skill born of the necessity to reach the beach before
half of Beirut was mobilized to seek them out. Amidst
blaring horns, flashing headlights and the shriek of
tires, the Citroën cleared the southern end of the Rue
Riad el-Solh turning on to a wide main road. There
was no obvious sign of pursuit.

Sitting motionless in the front passenger seat, Colonel Yaacobi still carried the carbine Marsh had given
him. Like the others in the car he remained silent, his
eyes flickering occasionally as the driver hurled the
Citroën through yet another gap in the hundreds of
cars crowding the highway.

For another twenty minutes five people held their
breath not daring to believe they could make it. It was
Yaacobi who spoke first.

"Slow down now," he said. "We will draw attention
to ourselves otherwise." Turning round in his seat he
inspected Marsh then moved his eyes to Sharmila saying something to her in Hebrew. She shook her head
then pulled open the neck of her blouse. A blood-
soaked dressing covered one shoulder.

Reaching for the adhesive tape holding the dressing
to her skin Marsh peeled it back. The edges raw and
livid, a terrible bloody slot had been torn three-quarters of an inch deep through the flesh beside her neck.
He replaced the covering gently.

"Cabinda is dead," he said to Yaacobi as if to explain.

The Colonel reached into his own shirt to pull out a
crumpled roll of paper.

"And I have the drawings, Steven."

"Dryden?" Marsh asked quietly.

The spotter with the injured face answered the question. "He died trying to kill the girl who was with us."

Marsh shuddered inwardly. If he had not learned at
the last minute that Sharmila might be in the hotel as
Cabinda's captive, he doubted if he could have forced
himself to play his part in such a brutal raid. He could

still not bring himself to believe she was sitting beside him and he was frightened at what yet could happen.

On the outskirts of Beirut now, traveling on bumpy unlit roads, the Citroën turned a sharp right-hand corner on the brow of a hill. A mile from them the Mediterranean stretched away into a starlit night appearing as a vast area of smooth darkness.

No one was prepared to communicate their hopes to the others in the car, each person praying the dinghies would be there and that they might still reach the beach without encountering resistance. Tension increased as the Citroën descended the hill.

For Marsh, weak from loss of blood and too exhausted to even contemplate a final disaster, traveling the last few miles to the coast seemed to take half a lifetime. Sharmila was alive, safe, alive and his. All they had to do was transfer from land to sea—and the promise of their dream could still come true. Only minutes from safety he hung on desperately to his hopes.

For Yaacobi the raid had been a further test of what he knew was a man too tired and too old to engage in such bloody violence. If the drawings had not been at stake he would never have been permitted to lead the mission, but Yaacobi knew now that whatever the stakes in the future he would never go on another. In the life of every man there comes a time when the limit has been reached and Colonel Yacobi was fully aware of how far the limit had been exceeded in the last hour. Like Marsh and the others he tried to believe he would return home to live out a life already half over.

Six minutes later the driver ran the front wheels of the Citroën into a sand dune beside a narrow track leading to the beach.

They threw open the doors then, half walking and half running, made the final effort to traverse the last fifty yards of their journey. Leaving Sharmila to assist the Colonel who, Marsh discovered had been badly wounded in the ankle, he supported himself between the driver and the surviving spotter.

As they reached the end of the track, black figures rose silently from the dunes. Outlined against the sand, their total blackness was both striking and sinister but Marsh had never been more glad to see anyone in his life.

Sheathed from head to foot in wet suits, the Israeli frogmen assisted what remained of the raiding party to the waiting dinghies.

One by one they fell gratefully on to the cool wet rubber floors, hardly able to believe it was finished and so exhausted that the drenching they received from the surf did nothing to revive them.

Like so many black seals which had risen to the surface, six Zodiac dinghies drew steadily away from the shores of Lebanon carrying their occupants out to the missile boats hiding in the darkness. Soon, any observers on the beach would need night binoculars to pick out the men who, such a short while before, had so viciously disrupted Beirut's night life.

Once on board the naval boats, the wounded were attended to whilst the powerful diesels were restarted. Then, heading out to sea, the two Israeli vessels disappeared into the furthest shadows of the Mediterranean before turning towards their home ports far away to the south.

Below decks in the lead boat, Sharmila was endeavoring to keep Marsh awake. He was very sleepy and very happy.

"Please tell me, Steven," she shook him. "I know you were looking for me—tell me how you knew. I want to know."

He propped himself up on his left elbow studying the face of the girl he loved. "Cabinda was greedy. He sent a letter to your government offering you back for fifty thousand American dollars. That's the trouble with kidnapers, they're not just greedy they're stupid, too. Who would pay that kind of dough for you?"

She opened her eyes wide. "If I'd known I could have told him Israel never pays ransom—not for anyone."

Marsh smiled at her. He wanted to kiss her again.

"Good job you didn't," he said. "Or he wouldn't have taken the trouble to export you from the States. I thought you were dead, brown eyes."

She shivered. "And I thought you were dead, too. But we're both alive." She touched his face.

Marsh was falling asleep again. This time she leaned over him and kissed him on the mouth. "We've got a lot to talk about," she whispered.

Once again Israel had paid in kind for a Palestinian raid on Tel Aviv. In the higher places of the Arab world, repercussions were already beginning for there were survivors on the third floor of the Liban hotel who were more than willing to tell of their miraculous escape.

Again a handful of Israeli guerrillas had extracted terrible retribution and this time the leaders of the PLO knew exactly why the location of the raid had been chosen so carefully. That the English president of the FAAC was dead with his accomplices was of no great consequence. That the Jews had escaped with the drawings of their homing missile was a blow after such protracted negotiations, but the boycott list could remain unaltered—be extended even, and Israel would gain nothing from the blood she had spilt tonight. Already the Arab press was making ready tomorrow's headlines condemning the Jewish raid.

And in Washington and in London instructions were going out to editors of Western newspapers to make sure not only that Israel's demands were met but that the oil-producing nations of the Middle East could not suspect active participation by either Britain or the United States.

Another exercise in diplomatic tightrope walking had begun and only a few men would ever know the truth behind the series of incidents which had precipitated the Israeli raid. Some of these men would remain in the service of their countries and in time perhaps remember nothing more than their own involvement in the affair. But for two very special people, whose lives had been so suddenly changed, it would be impossible to ever forget the strange and violent way that fate had brought them together.